SANDS OF
DUNE

THE DUNE SERIES

BY FRANK HERBERT

Dune
Dune Messiah
Children of Dune
God Emperor of Dune
Heretics of Dune
Chapterhouse: Dune

BY FRANK HERBERT, BRIAN HERBERT, AND KEVIN J. ANDERSON

The Road to Dune
(includes the original short novel *Spice Planet*)

BY BRIAN HERBERT AND KEVIN J. ANDERSON

Dune: House Atreides
Dune: House Harkonnen
Dune: House Corrino
Dune: The Butlerian Jihad
Dune: The Machine Crusade
Dune: The Battle of Corrin
Hunters of Dune
Sandworms of Dune
Paul of Dune
The Winds of Dune
Sisterhood of Dune
Mentats of Dune
Navigators of Dune
Tales of Dune
Dune: The Duke of Caladan
Dune: The Lady of Caladan
Dune: The Heir of Caladan
Sands of Dune

BY BRIAN HERBERT

Dreamer of Dune
(biography of Frank Herbert)

SANDS OF
DUNE

Brian Herbert
and
Kevin J. Anderson

TOR

A TOM DOHERTY ASSOCIATES BOOK
NEW YORK

SANDS OF DUNE

Copyright © 2022 by Herbert Properties LLC

"Blood of the Sardaukar" first published in *Unfettered III*, edited by Shawn Speakman, Grim Oak Press, 2018

"The Waters of Kanly" first published in *Infinite Stars*, edited by Bryan Thomas Schmidt, Titan Books, 2017

"Imperial Court" first published in *Unbound II*, edited by Shawn Speakman, Grim Oak Press, 2022

A Tor Book
Published by Tom Doherty Associates
120 Broadway
New York, NY 10271

www.tor-forge.com

Tor® is a registered trademark of Macmillan Publishing Group, LLC.

Library of Congress Cataloging-in-Publication Data

Names: Herbert, Brian, author. |
Anderson, Kevin J., author. | Herbert, Brian. Edge of a crysknife.
Title: Sands of Dune / Brian Herbert and Kevin J. Anderson.
Description: First edition. | New York : Tor, 2022. | Series: The Dune series |
"A Tom Doherty Associates book."
Identifiers: LCCN 2022007992 (print) | LCCN 2022007993 (ebook) |
ISBN 9781250805676 (hardcover) | ISBN 9781250805690 (ebook)
Subjects: LCSH: Dune (Imaginary place)—Fiction. |
LCGFT: Science fiction. | Novellas.
Classification: LCC PS3558.E617 S25 2022 (print) | LCC PS3558.E617 (ebook) |
DDC 813'.54—dc23/eng/20220302
LC record available at https://lccn.loc.gov/2022007992
LC ebook record available at https://lccn.loc.gov/2022007993

Our books may be purchased in bulk for promotional, educational, or business use. Please contact your local bookseller or the Macmillan Corporate and Premium Sales Department at 1-800-221-7945, extension 5442, or by email at MacmillanSpecialMarkets@macmillan.com.

First Edition: 2022

Printed in the United States of America

0 9 8 7 6 5 4 3 2 1

When we consider dedicating any book we have written, we always think first of the incredible women who have dedicated their entire lives to us, Janet Herbert and Rebecca Moesta. As part of our commitment to them, we lovingly dedicate this book to Janet and Rebecca.

And, in special gratitude for his extensive work in the Dune universe, we also want to dedicate Sands of Dune to Christopher Morgan of Tor Books for his constant support of this series.

Introduction

SANDS AND STORIES

Frank Herbert's original *Dune* is one of the first truly epic science fiction novels ever published in scope, theme, cast of characters—and in its sheer length.

He originally published the novel in three separate parts—*Book I "Dune," Book II "Muad'Dib,"* and *Book III "The Prophet"*—and at around two hundred thousand words it was a massive novel for the time, significantly longer than the average SF book, and considered unmarketable by Frank Herbert's agent and every publisher with the exception of one, Chilton Books.

Fortunately, that mindset has changed over time.

In the quarter century that we have been working together in the Dune universe, each Brian Herbert–Kevin J. Anderson novel has also been substantial in length, ranging from 130,000 to 240,000 words.

Over the course of building these complex epics with huge casts of characters, we've occasionally been intrigued by smaller ideas, interesting spotlights on tangential events, or vignettes that did not find a place inside the core novels. Sometimes we wanted to explore an interesting peripheral character or a loose story thread that would help flesh out the larger epic that now spans more than twenty novels.

The smaller stories are grains of sand, rather than towering dunes. But they still remain important elements in the Dune universe.

The first Dune short story we ever wrote together, in the late 1990s, was inspired by a close reading of a brief account in *Dune* about the battle of Arrakeen. During the violent overthrow of House Atreides, Baron Harkonnen uses archaic artillery weapons to blast at caves in the Shield Wall, where a group of Atreides soldiers had holed up. "The guns nibbled at the caves where the Duke's fighting men had retreated for a last-ditch stand. Slowly measured bites of orange glare, showers of rock and dust in the brief illumination—and the Duke's men were being sealed off to die by starvation, caught like animals in their burrows."

Our story "A Whisper of Caladan Seas" explores what happened to those doomed soldiers entombed in caves on a desert world far from their beloved oceans. What did they think about in their last moments? How did they hold themselves together while their air and water slowly ran out? That story was published in *Amazing Stories* magazine and is included in the collection *Tales of Dune*.

In our numerous rereads of the original novel, we kept finding intriguing side trips, questions that deserved to be answered in individual stories of their own.

For instance: ancient Shadout Mapes, the quiet, observant, and ultimately rebellious housekeeper in the Arrakeen Residency, who endured years and years of Harkonnen rule. Her long and eventful life is only briefly hinted at in her scenes in *Dune*, before she is murdered. We decided to tell part of her backstory, the origin of this brave Fremen woman and how she resisted Harkonnen rule through both violent and subtle means. We begin this new collection of stories with "The Edge of a Crysknife."

During the Battle of Arrakeen, after the Harkonnens have effectively conquered the city, Duke Leto has been captured and the Baron gloats over what he will do to his archenemy. One grim Sardaukar colonel bashar comes to the Baron and insists on the Emperor's orders that Duke Leto is to be treated with honor. "My Emperor has charged me to make certain his royal cousin dies cleanly without agony. . . . I'm to report to my Emperor what I see with my own eyes." This Sardaukar is quite determined to ensure that the Duke does not suffer any more than necessary.

We wondered about that Sardaukar officer's connection to Leto, his possible past experience with House Atreides. We also wanted to tell, for the first time ever, the background of the fearsome Sardaukar in a story of a young refugee boy inducted into the Sardaukar corps and trained to become a ruthless killer. Our tale about that, "Blood of the Sardaukar," is the second story in this book.

As the seeds of our story after that, a couple of years pass in *Dune* after Paul falls in among the Fremen and gradually becomes the legendary Muad'Dib. During that time, the troubadour-warrior Gurney Halleck is off stage—making his home, joining a band of smugglers, working with them in small guerilla operations against the hated Harkonnens. What adventures a man like Gurney Halleck must have had! We decided to explore those "lost years" in "The Waters of Kanly," the third story in this collection.

Finally, traveling to a different period ten thousand years earlier for our fourth story, we visited the tumultuous events not long after the end of the Butlerian Jihad, when the thinking machines had been overthrown and the Imperium was just being formed. The Corrino dynasty began to establish itself as the rulers of all humanity. In that time, the ruthless blood feud between House Atreides and House Harkonnen had already worked its way into the fabric of the Landsraad.

The wounds between Harkonnen and Atreides grow ever deeper. The last story in this collection, "Imperial Court"—set a few years after the end of *Navigators of Dune*—shows one more twist of that knife, and clears the way for an entirely new part of Dune history.

Sands of Dune collects these four tales, spanning Frank Herbert's Dune universe of thousands of years and a million worlds. This vast canvas has given us plenty of room and the creative freedom to tell a wide range of stories.

—Brian Herbert and Kevin J. Anderson

THE EDGE OF A CRYSKNIFE

I know that you have borne children, that you have lost loved ones, that you have hidden in fear and that you have done violence and will yet do more violence. I know many things.

—LADY JESSICA to Shadout Mapes

PART I

10,135 A.G.
56 years before *Dune*

I

Blood covered her hands, and when it dried in the hot desert air, Mapes regretted the waste of water. But that couldn't be helped—these men needed to die. They were Harkonnens.

In the heat of the deep desert, a huge spice harvester throbbed and thrummed as enormous treads crawled along the crest of a dune. Intake machinery chewed up the sand and digested the powder through a complex interplay of centrifuges and electromagnetic separators. The harvester vomited out a cloud of exhaust dust, sand, and debris that settled onto the disturbed dunes behind the moving machine, while the bins filled up with the rare spice melange.

The droning operation sent pulsing vibrations beneath the desert, sure to call a sandworm . . . and very soon. The noise also drowned out the sounds of Fremen violence inside the great machine.

In the operations bridge of the moving factory, another Harkonnen worker tried to flee, but a Fremen death-commando, a Fedaykin, ran after him. Disguised in a grimy shipsuit, the attacker had predatory and sure movements, not at all like the morose sand crew the Harkonnens had hired.

Though small and brown-skinned, young Mapes had fit in among the regular workers, as had her companions, but she didn't laugh or joke with the sand crew, didn't try to make friends with people she knew she would have to kill. Nevertheless, she and her companions were hired by uninquisitive company bosses. Too many crews had been lost as it was, some through desertion, others through accidents and catastrophic loss in the field. Mapes knew that part of those losses were intentional—thanks to freedom fighters like herself.

Her companion Ahar, a muscular man of few words but great

dedication, slammed the doomed worker against a metal bulkhead and raised his crysknife—a milky crystalline blade ground from the discarded tooth of a giant worm—and drove the point deep into the man's throat. The victim gurgled, but did not scream as he slid to the deck. Ahar had used an instinctive Fremen killing blow, one that brought quick and silent death, but wasted no more blood than was necessary.

Alas, today the commandos would not reclaim the water of these victims for the tribe. They had to kill the crew, destroy the spice harvester, and escape like dust devils in the wind. There was no time.

Mapes gripped her own knife, a razor-sharp weapon made of simple plasteel. Possessing a crysknife was a sacred honor, and her comrades in the sietch had not yet deemed her worthy of one, though she had already participated in more than a dozen raids.

Mapes was a firebrand, but Fremen women did not usually join the Fedaykin, the special death commando squads that were historically formed to avenge particular wrongs—and the very existence of these offworld oppressors on Dune was *wrong*. The Fedaykin had accepted Mapes in part because of her skill and tenacity, but primarily due to her legendary mother. Some saw Mapes as a new Safia, and they were willing to let her prove herself.

Now, the young woman pursued her second victim inside the noisy operations bridge. Five workers lay dead already, smearing the dusty metal of the deck with their blood. Although she was smaller than her target, the spice worker was afraid. She collided with him and knocked him against the bank of controls. He defended himself like one who had never been in a fight before. He flailed his hands to drive her off, and she slashed open his palm with the edge of her knife. He gasped and doubled over, more in horror than in pain.

"Why? Why are you doing this?" he bleated. "We paid your wages! We just harvest the spice."

"You are Harkonnens," she said. "All Harkonnens must die."

The man swiped at her with his bleeding hand, flinging droplets of red through the air like precious rain. "Not a Harkonnen! Never even met Dmitri Harkonnen! Just an offworld hire brought in to work the machinery. My contract is up in six months." He stared at his dead comrades on the deck. "None of us are Harkonnens."

"You work for the enemy, therefore you are the enemy." Without further conversation, she stabbed him and shoved him aside, then turned to work the controls. She shut down the main engines, and the lumbering factory ground to a halt in a valley between dunes. The intake scoop and the turbine blades creaked and froze silent; the gray-tan exhaust plume dissipated.

Increasingly urgent voices came over the outside commline. "Wormsign spotted. Range, four minutes, twenty seconds. Prepare for retrieval."

Mapes considered just ignoring the call, but decided to continue the deception. She flicked on the comm. "Acknowledged. Preparing evacuation parties. Send in the carryall."

Hearing a yell behind her, Mapes whirled as a uniformed factory worker threw himself at her with desperation in his eyes. She raised her blade to defend herself, but his feet stuttered and stumbled on the deck. Behind him, another man plunged a crysknife into his back, pushed deeper, harder, until the worker crumpled.

She saw the rakish, handsome face of her rescuer, and her heart swelled. "Thank you Rafir, my love. I will reward you later when we are back home in the sietch."

Her partner, heart of her heart, took charge of the Fedaykin band, who were now the only survivors on the operations bridge. "Hai ha—time to go! Our enemies are dead, and Mapes shut down the machinery. And a worm comes!"

The other Fremen took this as good news and cheered. "Shai-Hulud!"

"Shai-Hulud," Mapes responded. The monstrous sandworm would do the rest of the work for them, cleansing the sands.

Leaving the dead behind with a whispered regret of wasted water, Mapes, Rafir, and their companions emerged from the roof access hatch to the open, dusty air, and climbed down rungs along the great factory's hull. The smell of acrid cinnamon—potent, fresh melange—filled the air. An exposed spice vein formed a rusty stain

across the sand, worth millions of solaris to offworlders. Now that
fortune would all go back into the sands of Dune where it belonged.

Outside, three groundcars rolled along the powdery surface, ex-
terior teams rushing back toward the harvester for extraction and
rescue along with the cargo. The commline was scratchy with static
caused by the disturbed sand and dust, and the voices were tinged
with fear. "A worm is coming. Less than three minutes! Why didn't
you sound the return call?"

An overlapping voice bellowed, "Chief, why aren't you re-
sponding?"

A third said, "Carryall's coming. I see it in the air. We can make
it back to the harvester pickup point, but just barely."

Climbing down the hot rungs, Mapes looked down at Rafir. They
exchanged a smile as sharp as a crysknife's edge. Reaching the soft
ground, Mapes stripped out of the despised company uniform and
tossed it into the hot desert wind. The other commandos did the
same as if they felt soiled. Underneath, they all wore stillsuits that
modulated their body temperatures in the heat and reclaimed all of
the body's lost moisture. Mapes pulled forth a line with connected
noseplugs from her collar and inserted them in her nostrils.

With spare, efficient movements, the Fedaykin circled behind
the enormous machine and worked their way up the rising face of
the nearby dune. Despite her small size, Mapes kept up, and the
team respected her. She had as much drying blood on her hands as
her companions did on theirs.

Up in the sky, she spotted the glint of sunlight on metal, the
rescue craft swooping in. The carryall was designed to connect with
the spice factory and lift it to safety when a ubiquitous, destructive
sandworm arrived. The three groundcars raced toward the factory,
ready to be taken away, but the workers would find no refuge.

The band of Fremen climbed the crumbling dune face, not both-
ering to disguise the vibrations of their footsteps because there was
simply so much background noise in the excavation area. On the
sand crest ahead, Mapes could see a lone, huddled figure. Rafir spotted him as well. "Onorio is in position," he said.

The carryall swooped in, a large framework with powerful beating wings. Mapes paused to glance at the sand workers scrambling

out of their groundcars, waving their hands at the approaching rescue craft.

Out beyond the harvested area, she saw ripples in the sand, a swift behemoth coming closer and closer. The timing would be tight.

On the crest of the dune, Onorio rose to his feet, discarding all pretense of camouflage. He shook dust from his tan cape and raised a long weapon, bracing it against his shoulder. An archaic device that one of the disguised Fremen had purchased from a rarities dealer in Arrakeen, considered nothing more than a useless curiosity in a city where most people wore shields. But out here in the open desert, shields were far more problematic, and the weight of a shield generator would be too much for a carryall and its gigantic load. Mapes paused to watch what the antique weapon would do.

The rocket launcher coughed out a projectile that arced upward, deceptively silent, but when it struck the unshielded carryall, the explosion blossomed into smoke and fire. The retrieval craft broke apart, and smoking shrapnel thundered down like meteor strikes. One of the fragments crashed into a groundcar, killing two workers who tried to dive out of the way.

The retreating Fedaykin reached the dune crest, and Rafir congratulated Onorio on his shot. Only three members of the harvester crew remained alive, and after the destruction of the carryall, they huddled in despair by their groundcars, knowing their fate when the great worm arrived.

Like a thick, tan storm-front, the ripples in the sand approached. The worm exploded to the surface, a leviathan of crusted rings with an open, round mouth as vast as the largest grotto in a Fremen sietch. The crystalline teeth lining its gullet looked like tiny silver thorns.

Drawn by the vibrations, offended by trespassers in the sand, Shai-Hulud ran amuck. Though transfixed by the sandworm's strength and majesty, Mapes fully understood the danger. She felt like a shivering rodent, hypnotized by a viper about to strike.

Rafir touched her arm. "Come, we must use the tumult as our opportunity." He released a deep breath before fitting his nose plugs and tightening his stillsuit fittings. "Our lives depend on it. We have to go to ground."

The sandworm crashed into the motionless harvester, pulling

the huge factory under the sands along with its full bins of melange. It also destroyed all trace of the ruined carryall, the abandoned groundcars, and the workers.

The Fedaykin rolled down the other side of the tall dune like discarded debris, and when they were far down the sloping face, they each checked their breathing tubes and mouth coverings, pulled hooded cloaks over their bodies, and wallowed into the sand.

Covered by a layer of dust, Mapes lay perfectly still, trying not to breathe, willing her heartbeat to slow. They had vanished into the sand, but the worm did not use eyes. She couldn't see anything, but she knew her fellow Fremen were there, Rafir was there, and Shai-Hulud continued his blessed destruction.

Many hours later, after the worm retreated to the depths of the desert, Mapes and her friends would emerge. After nightfall and the rising of the two moons, they would make their way back to the sietch.

Mapes couldn't wait to tell her mother of another victory against the Harkonnens.

II

The sietch welcomed the Fedaykin as heroes. When the door-seals were closed so that no moisture would leak from the hidden warren of caves, Mapes and Rafir removed their nose plugs and mouth coverings, peeled away forehead pads that reclaimed every pearl of sweat. The stillsuit was like a second skin, but when she removed the garment and donned looser sietch clothes, she felt as if she became a different person. She stepped into the crowded bustle of community activity.

A comforting chatter of conversation rolled around her ears, like sands whispering across the open bled. The thick sietch odors had a texture of their own, a raucous symphony of strong but familiar smells. Outsiders would have found the stench unbearable, but Mapes inhaled a deep breath, identifying the undertones of old sweat and dust, the residue of volatile fuels, acrid lubricants for moving parts, raw plastics and chemical explosives, and under it all the ubiquitous hint of melange. She heard the clack and swish of looms as older women wove durable spice-fiber cloth. The Fremen community was a smoothly functioning machine, not unlike the spice harvester the commandos had destroyed.

Outside along the ridge, teams built, installed, or fixed windtraps and dew collectors to steal the tiniest amounts of water vapor from the air. Some people manufactured and fitted new stillsuits, while others repaired them. A stillsuit was life; a stillsuit was survival. Offworlder fools fabricated their own poor-quality stillsuits in the cities, but those garments were made with little understanding of the needs of the desert. Even greater fools bought such stillsuits and believed them to be safe.

The rest of the Fedaykin, all men, changed together, and Mapes was waiting for Rafir when he emerged. As the two walked deeper into the sietch, excited tales rushed ahead of them. Onorio and Ahar waved as the people cheered another successful blow against Governor Dmitri Harkonnen. The naib of the sietch had already released extra quantities of melange and fresh spice beer for the people.

Someone thrust a narrow-mouthed flask into Rafir's hands as he walked past. He took a swig, closed his eyes, let out a sigh, and then handed the flask to Mapes, since no one had offered her one. He took another container of spice beer for himself. Young Fremen women followed the returning Fedaykin, some with demure glances, others bold and flirtatious. Onorio already had a young woman on each arm, and Ahar was trying to steal one of them away from him. "One shot with that old gadget," Onorio boasted. "Blasted the carryall out of the sky! It was the most beautiful thing."

Mapes clung to Rafir and dismissed the other laughing girls. Every woman in the sietch knew that if they tried to seduce Mapes's man, they would find a knife at their throats. Laughing, Rafir slid his arm around her waist. "Hai ha! Your jealousy makes my desire for you even hotter!"

"Fremen have learned not to let anyone steal what is ours." She pulled him closer.

In a general mood of release, the people ate honeyed wafers and melange cakes, drank spice beer and even stronger spice liquor. With their normally hard lives, the Fremen would release their tensions and spend their energies in whatever joyous manner they chose. The naib understood her tribe and gave them the space to do what they needed.

Mapes and Rafir finished their flasks at the same time, and she felt the warmth and energy combine with a fuzziness that blurred her inhibitions. She led the young man to their private chamber, a stone-walled alcove with a privacy curtain of spice fiber. Rafir's words were slightly slurred as the spice beer took hold. "Before we have our own celebration, should we not see—"

"I will meet with her later." Mapes took his hand, leading him into the alcove. "You are more important."

Once they were alone, Mapes felt the roar of passion consuming her. She kissed him and pulled him to her. Mapes stopped thinking about the successful raid and what she would tell her mother about it . . .

AN HOUR LATER, both exhausted and energized from the effects from the spice and the lovemaking, Mapes went to see her mother, Safia, naib of the sietch.

She stood at the hanging glass beads that adorned the chamber doorway. Incense burners added yet another layer of scent to the recycled sietch air. Naib Safia sat on her specially made chair, a mature woman with her aba hood pulled back to show rich, auburn hair streaked with coppery highlights. Safia had designed her own distinctive outfit to mark the respect due to her as a revered mother among the tribe, combined with the male trappings of a typical naib. Safia was an exception to almost every Fremen custom.

The older woman sat up straight in her chair as Mapes let the softly clicking bead curtain fall behind her. Self-consciously, Safia pulled dark skirts over her knees to cover the stump of her left leg. Her hated prosthetic limb was propped against her chair, to be donned only when necessary. "I heard of your adventure, Daughter. You will grow as great as me one day. For now I am content to live vicariously through your battles." The wistful flicker that crossed her expression belied her words.

"Our fight for freedom continues." Mapes came forward and bowed. "Part of the success belongs to you, Naib. You blessed the plan."

"Why so formal? We are here in private. Tell me everything that happened." Safia's sparkling, blue-within-blue eyes showed a lifetime of spice consumption.

Mapes took a step closer to the chair, which seemed both a nest and a throne. "When you fought alongside the Fedaykin and tricked them into accepting you, Mother, you told me that you succeeded only because you never showed them your soft side. Every day is a battle, you said. Men were assumed to be equal, while women had to prove it."

"And I did prove it, Daughter, as will you. I carved one stone step on the cliff you have to climb, but you must carve the next one on your own, and someone else will do the next. It is a long, steep climb up that rock face." Her mother's face became wistful. "At least you do not have to pretend when you go out on raids. You are who you are."

Mapes bowed. "I am what you made me."

"In part," Safia agreed.

"In part." Together, they both muttered a brief benediction in the old language of Chakobsa.

When her mother was a young woman, defiant and violent, she had created a false Fremen identity for herself, claiming to be a youth named Iber from another sietch. Safia had tied a tight band around her breasts to hide her shape, kept her face scuffed and dirty, her stillsuit hood up. She joined the commandos on raids, killing the lumbering watchdogs from House Richese, the previous planetary governors before the Harkonnens.

After her twelfth raid and a kill count of more than thirty, the doddering old naib at the time, a man full of fire and false expectations, championed "Iber" and presented the hero with a sacred crysknife. Accepting, she held the sandworm tooth high among the cheering Fremen as they welcomed their new tribe member. Then Safia pulled down the stillsuit hood shook loose her copper-streaked dark hair. The people muttered, confused. She called out, "I am Safia! You know me, but you underestimate me."

Some of the older men were indignant, offended. One fool even had the gall to blurt out, "A woman cannot be a Fedaykin commando."

Safia had rounded on the man, pointing her milky crysknife at him. "Ask the thirty dead Richesian dogs. Does a starving person turn away food that is right in front of him? Does a person fighting for his life cast aside a weapon that is right at hand?"

Some tribe members were convinced, while others continued to complain until Safia confronted the fool who voiced the bitterest complaints. She challenged him to a duel, on the spot. "Let me blood my new crysknife!" Aggressively, she pressed forward, eager to use her weapon, and the fool had backed down. No one else challenged her.

From that time, Safia had led countless more commando raids that struck Richesian operations and ruined countless melange stockpiles, finally driving out House Richese. Emperor Elrood IX could no longer tolerate the incompetence and the loss of spice revenue, so he ousted the Richesians. A victory for Safia. But the Harkonnens had proved no better.

"I raised you to this life, Mapes, dearest to my heart." She chuckled to herself. "When I talk of my raids, you must think it merely the melancholy nostalgia of someone whose fires are fading."

"Not fading, Mother!" Mapes said, then quickly bowed and remembered to use the proper title. "*Naib*. Every one of your stories inspired me, made me want to do the same." She straightened with pride. "And I am doing so. This raid was our greatest yet, but not my last. You were my mentor. You trained me to become your equal someday."

Safia reached out to pat Mapes's forearm in a warm maternal gesture. "You will never be my equal, child. You will be *yourself*. That is the best anyone can hope for . . . and your best may be better than mine, in your own way."

Emotions formed a lump in Mapes's throat, and she turned away. "We should go to the sietch gathering. The people will be waiting to hear from us. You must address the tribe and tell them what has occurred."

"Your young Rafir is already telling them stories." Safia's voice grew more serious. "I am not finished speaking with you yet. There is one more thing you must learn. You cannot imitate me. I proved to the Fremen that a woman could fight just as hard as any Fedaykin, and be as deadly. Typically, we are vicious on the battlefield, but in a way different from the men. I proved we could be exactly the same."

"The Fedaykin treat me no differently," Mapes said. "Some may still doubt me in private, but free people are allowed to think stupid things."

"That is not what I mean. I fought with them on countless raids, killed many enemies. I became the bane of House Richese . . . until my accident." She placed a palm on the sudden angle in her folded skirts where her left leg ended.

During a bold raid, Safia and a group of Fremen warriors had ridden a sandworm to one of the spice operation outposts. But the worm had gone wild, and Safia tangled her boot in a mounting rope as she tried to leap from the creature's back. The worm rolled, crushing her leg. She had slashed the rope with her crysknife and tumbled away, somehow surviving, buried in sand until her comrades saved her. They had amputated Safia's leg. She had recovered, still vociferous and determined, but unable to accomplish what she had done before.

Nevertheless, Safia was legendary, revered, and when the previous old naib died coughing in his sleep, the sietch had acclaimed her to be their new leader. Since that time, Safia had been one of the most effective naibs among the Fremen.

"Just because you can do exactly the same things as a man, does not mean you should forget certain advantages you have as a woman. Not just in Fremen society but in the cities and towns, even where Harkonnen troops walk the streets. Use that weapon as well."

The suggestion made Mapes pause. She still felt the warm afterglow inside, the pleasurable throbbing from her lovemaking, but she took offense. She remembered the other young women easily seducing some of the Fedaykin. Mapes knew she was young, and many would find her attractive. Was that what her mother wanted her to do? With Harkonnens? "You ask me to go among the Harkonnens and . . . and be their whore?" Her eyes flared.

Safia gave her a steady gaze. "Your body is your own, and you do with it as you choose. Neither I nor any other person can order you to cheapen yourself." Her expression softened. "No, I meant something else, Daughter. In our society and among the offworlders, women have a singular unacknowledged advantage." She whispered the words as if they were a great secret. "They *underestimate* us. They do not see us. If you play your role correctly, you can be invisible . . . and an invisible person can accomplish great things."

She let that sink in before continuing. "If a Fremen man were to go to the Harkonnen residency in Carthag with a false identity and a menial job, they would be suspicious of him, accuse him of being a spy. A man couldn't hide it—but a *woman* with the proper meek demeanor, unobtrusive garb, and solicitous attitude could walk among them, watch, and learn. Such a person could become a treasure trove of information."

Mapes was surprised. "Meek and unobtrusive? You know what I've done, the raids I've fought, the people I've killed. You think I can be quiet and shy?"

"I did not tell you to be any such thing, Daughter! I told you to *act* like that. Spies can also be warriors." Safia's deep blue eyes grew more intense. "There is something I want you to learn from Dmitri Harkonnen, something important, and we will all use the information you have found."

The naib reached into the folds of her skirts and withdrew a long object in a curved sheath. It had a worn hilt, and Safia drew it partially out to reveal a milky-white blade. Mapes felt her heart skip a beat. "I want you to have this. You have earned it. Keep your plasteel blade, because there are many ways to kill the enemy and no one can have enough weapons, but this crysknife will be the blade of your heart, the blade of your soul."

"Your *crysknife*, Mother!"

Safia extended it to her, pressed it into her hands. "*Your* crysknife, Mapes."

In wonder Mapes touched the hilt, began to draw the knife further, but Safia stopped her. "If drawn, that knife must not be sheathed without blood. You know the way. Do you intend to kill someone today?"

Mapes stared at the partially exposed white blade, as if hypnotized. The edge itself seemed to demand blood payment. She pushed it back into its sheath with a *snik*, then pressed the knife to her breast, feeling the warmth and importance there. She looked at her mother. "Thank you."

"Make your own legend, my daughter."

Breaking the tense sincerity of the moment, Safia struggled to raise herself up with her arm, climbing to one foot. She indicated the prosthetic limb propped against her chair. "Now help me put this damned thing on so I can address the people."

THE ENTIRE SIETCH came together to acknowledge the Fed-aykin victory. The naib stood in an alcove high up the grotto wall, where the acoustics amplified her words. "Tonight many Harkon-nens are dead or hurting. One of their expensive spice harvesters has been demolished, their crew slain, the entire cargo destroyed. Oh, that will sting them like a scorpion."

One man in the crowd let out a loud hoot. Mapes recognized Onorio.

Safia continued, "And we will keep striking them, raiding them, inflicting pain on them." The background murmur rose to an en-thusiastic cheer. The melange they had all consumed drew the tribe together, made them stronger. "We will be like grains of sand in a Coriolis wind that can scour the flesh from bones." The tribe roared with more enthusiasm. "Sooner or later, Dmitri Harkonnen will also pack up and leave in shame. The Padishah Emperor will pull him away, just as he did with the Richesians." Safia raised her arms, and the gathered people were enthralled.

But one dissenting voice called out, "Then what? Will we finally be free?"

"We already cast out House Richese," she said. "We proved our strength."

"And then we got the Harkonnens," the man replied. "When Dmitri Harkonnen goes away, what if the next one is worse?"

"It cannot be," Mapes shouted beside her mother. "It cannot be! We must pray that the next one will be better, until someday they are gone entirely, leaving us with our own world. Dune!"

Cheers drowned out the dissenting voices. Safia placed a hand on her daughter's shoulder. It looked to all the others like a reassur-ing gesture, though the naib was bracing herself on her awkward prosthetic leg. She raised her voice. "On that matter, Mapes and I have a plan."

III

Despite her initial skepticism, she discovered a different method of fighting, a new way to resist the Harkonnen oppressors. With her mother's careful advice and instruction, Mapes learned the value of stealth over outright destruction.

Soon enough, she realized that she was good at it.

Carthag was a raw, new city of metal and plaz, built with brute force by Dmitri Harkonnen. The previous Richesian governors had established a secondary urban center there, but by tradition had kept their planetary operations in the older city of Arrakeen. Dmitri wanted to establish a new, muscular Harkonnen headquarters that looked more like Harko City on his home planet of Giedi Prime.

Once she received her specific mission from Naib Safia, Mapes immersed herself among the nondescript people of Carthag. She spent a few weeks creating a life and an identity there, but these townspeople were not Fremen and did not have a fire in their eyes. She found them hopeless and trapped, forced to depend on the bleak safety net of the spice industry.

Mapes studied them, learned how to act and dress like them. She used her newfound skill to become invisible. Before long she had secured herself a position on the Harkonnen household staff.

Some months earlier, after consuming too much spice beer in a Carthag tavern, a Harkonnen guard had let slip the information that regular illicit spice shipments were prepared for secret delivery to House Mutelli, an under-the-table sale that bypassed the usual imperial taxes. Safia received this information with great interest, realizing that if her Fedaykin could destroy that shipment, it would cost Dmitri Harkonnen dearly—and because the deal was illegal in the first place, the siridar governor could not lodge an official complaint. Safia wanted to know the details of what the Harkonnens were doing, the location of the shipments, how often they occurred and when, and how the Fedaykin could destroy the operation.

Mapes would get that information.

Inside the looming Harkonnen mansion, the staff worked under layers of authority and supervision, a hierarchy of importance. Mapes pretended to follow the rules, while ignoring them in her heart. She performed her assigned duties, kept her eyes downcast, remained submissive and silent, yet her senses were attuned with all the alertness of a desert predator. No one gave her any particular notice; few bothered to learn her name.

Finding a way to work in the governor's offices, in close proximity to Dmitri Harkonnen himself, proved less difficult than she had expected. Many staff members had not only lost their employment but also their lives when they failed to meet the governor's expectations. The staff was afraid to serve in Dmitri's presence, melting away when the chief housekeeper asked for volunteers to fill the position. With only a limited time to discover details about the Mutelli black-market spice shipment, Mapes offered her services, much to the surprise of the chief housekeeper, a stern, short-haired woman who frowned at her, puckered her lips. "Why would you want to do that?"

"Did you not ask for a volunteer?"

"I did. And now I ask for your reasons."

Though Naib Safia wanted her daughter to be invisible, now Mapes feigned ambition and independence. She raised her chin, met the chief housekeeper's gaze. "None of us has a future on Arrakis, honored one, but if there are any opportunities at all, they lie in attracting the governor's notice." She sniffed. "I am good, I know it. Perhaps if I am fortunate, he will rely on me and promote me."

The chief housekeeper was surprised at her audacity. "You want to steal my job, then?"

"I want something important. I want a chance, a future. There are many other positions besides yours."

The chief housekeeper assessed her with stern skepticism, before her expression softened. "We shall see. One name is ahead of yours on the assignment list, but things may change in six months or a year. Be patient."

Mapes bowed in deference and left. She did not have six months or a year.

Easily enough, she learned the name of the person ahead of her on the assignment sheet, an unlikable older woman who had spent years in the Carthag mansion with little to show for it. She was not well liked, having adopted the Harkonnen ways of sneaky behavior and spreading malicious rumors. Mapes carried her crysknife carefully hidden, tied to her chest. She had expected a more dramatic way of blooding the revered blade for the first time, but this was necessary for the Fremen cause. She hunted down the bitter old woman alone at night in the back streets of Carthag, working on some unknown scheme, and stabbed her with the crysknife, then discarded her body in the shadows.

When the woman's death was discovered, it raised further alarm among the household staff, striking fear in the hearts of those who worked near the governor. Mapes found herself assigned without objection to duties in the business offices of Dmitri Harkonnen.

Within a few days Mapes caught her first sight of the governor, when she was instructed to deliver a tray with an open pitcher of water and a crystal goblet, signs of wealth and extravagance. She could smell the moisture as she carried the tray, careful not to spill a drop.

The governor took no notice of Mapes when she set the tray on the corner of his Elaccan bloodwood desk, which must have cost its weight in water just to ship here. The governor busied himself with plans and calculations, staring at his records with such intensity that implied he trusted no one else to make important decisions or allocations. Each time he shifted an object on the polished bloodwood, the living fluid inside the grain spread out in swirling, fractal patterns of deep crimson.

She made a slight cough in a dry throat, and he glanced up. He looked at her with dead, blue-gray eyes, and she was sure he didn't see *her*, merely an object, a moving piece of machinery that served a purpose. He looked back down at his work, and she departed as swiftly as possible.

Though Mapes was mostly insignificant among the household staff, she had the mindset of a predator as she assessed the offices, the records, and the governor himself. Dmitri Harkonnen was an angry, hungry man who wrapped himself in his status and fed on the fear he could inspire. In her first encounter with him, Mapes had learned the layout of his personal office and how he reacted to an interruption. She would discover more about him in the next days. Each little detail was one more step in the plan.

She wasn't sent back to the governor's office for two more days. Dmitri Harkonnen interacted little with the servants, except when something displeased him. Murmurs went through the staff when a manservant was summarily executed because he had not properly prepared the governor's clothing.

Twice more, Mapes was brought in to clean the governor's shelves, dust the floor, and replenish his pitcher of water. At no time did he greet, scold, or notice her at all. Despite the ambitions she had revealed to the chief housekeeper, the young woman remained unobtrusive, did not try to curry favor with him, but she gathered more details about Dmitri Harkonnen every time she entered his presence.

On her fourth assignment, she entered the main office to find no sign of Dmitri Harkonnen, the bloodwood desk empty. She had orders to polish the desk until it gleamed, and Mapes went about her work with the rag and polishing oil—next to the documents he had left out.

Vigorously cleaning the wood, she stole a glance, careful not to move anything, terrified and intent. She found a calendar entry, a date, the name of an isolated, rarely used landing field, and the word *Mutelli.*

After searching for weeks for even the faintest clue, she was startled to discover the precise knowledge she needed. Dmitri Harkonnen had perimeter security around the mansion and countless soldiers throughout Carthag, but he must have considered his household staff invisible, exactly as Safia suggested. The governor did not bother to *see* Mapes, but she spotted the critical information he had left vulnerable.

The following day Mapes slipped away from the governor's mansion and disappeared, never returning to her duties. It was time to assume her other role, one that was not quiet and meek.

IV

Returning to the sietch, Mapes became a different person again, her other self—her real self.

The naib and the Fedaykin received her stolen information with exhilaration, their rich blood on fire with the possibilities of a truly devastating strike against the Harkonnens.

Naib Safia had lurched up from her expanded chair on one foot to grab Mapes, pulling her into an embrace. She showed great pride in her daughter's accomplishment. "We have them now! You obtained vital information in a way that few others could." Safia's eyes narrowed. "I told you that we have an unrecognized power. Do not forget it."

"I did what you asked, Mother. I used stealth and cleverness instead of violence. I learned what we needed." She hardened her expression as she stepped away, not thinking of the older woman as her mother but as the leader of the tribe. "Now though, it is time for blood."

In their own private chamber, Rafir welcomed her back with childlike delight, and they made love with a passion she had not experienced before. Afterward, he said, "I had to prove I missed you!"

"This is a much more pleasant assignment." They held each other behind their spice fiber curtain.

Armed with detailed information about the illicit spice shipments, the Fedaykin made strategic plans. The isolated outpost was tucked into a sandy, crooked arm of Sihaya Ridge, several hours flight from the main Carthag spaceport. Fremen scouts had already observed the landing field, took note of the lookouts and defenses. A well-timed, coordinated strike could cause a great deal of damage and embarrassment to Dmitri Harkonnen and expose his black-market dealings to the Emperor.

On the day before the anticipated shipment, the Fedaykin donned stillsuits, gathered packs, hand weapons, and chemical explosives developed in the sietch. Mapes fitted the hood over her short hair, tightened her seals, smoothed the pad over her forehead. She and Rafir checked each other's fittings, their knives. Mapes lashed the prized crysknife to her side where she could easily draw it. The milky worm-tooth blade would taste Harkonnen blood before the end of the raid, a more worthy blooding. Rafir gave her his rakish grin, touched his own crysknife and nodded.

She was bursting to tell him her other news, her special news, but she would wait. If he noticed her foolish grin, he said nothing. Rafir led them all through the moisture-seal doors, and the Fedaykin set off.

Out on the dunes, they summoned one sandworm, which they rode for many hours, and then another, traveling hard across the open desert. Well before they were within sight of the base, they dismounted the last worm and allowed it to return and sulk beneath the sands. Arriving just beyond Sihaya Ridge during a long and colorful twilight, the commandos waited for full dark.

The Fedaykin approached on foot over the sand, moving carefully, then they lay prone on a rise above the secure Harkonnen landing field surrounded by low ridges of rock. In silence, they watched the movements, saw Harkonnen soldiers patrolling the perimeter, and whispered to one another as they revised the plan.

Mapes was ready to fight, feeling much more alive than when she had skulked around inside the Carthag mansion. Now, though, in these quiet moments, she decided it was time. She had more to tell Rafir, a personal secret she'd been waiting to share with him, and there could be no more perfect moment than now.

Seconds passed like sand grains falling down a dune face. Unable to contain herself any longer, she nudged Rafir as the tension hung in the air. "I have something for you, a gift."

He turned to her, his mind focused on the imminent attack, but when he saw her expression, he gave her all his attention. "What is it? What kind of gift?"

"A gift we made together, my love. I did not want to tell you until I was sure, but now I know. A second heart beats within me. You and I will have a child, another fighter to free our people and our world."

Rafir's expression filled with joy. "Hai ha!" With great effort, he restrained himself from leaping into the air. "That gives me the energy to kill ten more Harkonnens this night!" He spoke in a guarded whisper, just loud enough for the Fedaykin to hear. "Mapes and I will have a child!"

Ahar grunted a deep-throated laugh. "Then the Harkonnens will never be able to withstand us."

Onorio adjusted his pack of weapons. "That is one more thing to celebrate tonight when we get back to the sietch."

Rafir drew his crysknife and held it in front of Mapes. She unsheathed her own sacred weapon, letting the blue-white blade gleam in the light of the two small moons. "We will blood these before they are sheathed again." Rafir touched his edge to hers. "You are mine, Mapes, and I am yours."

"A wedding vow?" She felt warm inside. "I propose we have a better ceremony later."

"Agreed. But tonight we have killing to do."

Down in a basin protected by a rugged arm of rock, nine spice silos stood tall, illuminated by large, harsh glowglobes. Low barracks housed Harkonnen troops and base workers. The perimeter barricades looked ominous, but they were incomplete, more for show than for actual protection. Security at the Sihaya Ridge outpost depended more on desert isolation than on personnel and fences.

A broad, flat area of fused sand inside the rock-bounded complex served as a landing field. A blocky-looking cargo transport rested there with hatches open, its loading bay exposed to the night. Mapes knew this was the vessel that would carry the illicit spice. Tonight, she and her comrades would destroy that spice, kill the Harkonnen troops, and leave this outpost in ruins.

"They only outnumber us three to one," Onorio estimated. "This will be easy!"

Rafir chuckled. "Any day when I cannot kill three Harkonnens is a lazy day indeed."

"I see no shields," Ahar said, using oil-lens binoculars. He adjusted them, zoomed in. "Damnable shields."

Rafir made a disgusted noise. "Imagine the first time some fool used a shield close to the sands. That rocky bulwark protects them, but not from a maddened worm!"

"Our explosives will be acceptable," Mapes said.

As the darkness thickened, the commandos glided forward on footsteps as silent as blowing dust. Their stillsuits and cloaks were the color of sand mottled with shadows, making them invisible in the gloom.

Rafir sprinted to the rocky reef that marked the edge of the base, slipped behind one of the patrolling scouts and surprised him. He slashed the man's throat and let him fall without a sound. Two more Harkonnen guards turned and spotted the moving figures, but Fedaykin fell upon them before they could react, stabbing, and stabbing again to make sure. Moving beyond the perimeter rocks, the entire group pressed deeper into the base.

Mapes surprised a Harkonnen spice worker as he emerged from a reclamation latrine, and she felt a rush of satisfaction when her new blade slid like warm honey into the man's vital organs. She let his jerking body hang there for an extra moment, relishing the sensation, then she yanked her crysknife free and ran onward as he fell.

Rafir and five commandos headed toward the spice silos, ready with their most destructive sabotage. As planned, Mapes ran toward the cargo transport on the paved landing field. She would steal the clumsy vehicle as their escape craft, although they hoped to kill all of the Harkonnens. If they succeeded they would have all the time they could want.

Onorio and Ahar removed chemical explosives from their packs and headed toward the barracks. They would murder the hated soldiers while they slept, enthralled with their evil dreams. Fremen preferred to kill more intimately, using knives that could penetrate body shields, if necessary, but when three Harkonnens emerged from the barracks and one blurted out an alarm, the commandos used Maula pistols. With a *snap-click*, the projectile weapons killed the soldiers.

"No more time for stealth!" Mapes cried. She had almost reached the open hatch of the cargo transport.

Rafir bellowed out as he reached the first spice silo. "Hai ha! You know what to do."

Ahar and Onorio activated their grenades and tossed them onto the barracks rooftops. Explosions rumbled through the prefabricated buildings, and the barracks collapsed in flames. Several Harkonnens crawled out screaming, covered with a jelly of fire.

An odd sense of concern hovered just outside her conscious thoughts, however. Mapes spotted fewer troops than she expected. Could the Harkonnens really keep such minimal staff here with so many spice silos? And given the rock walls, did they truly need to abandon their shields? Large ones, maybe, but even personal shields? Arrogance! Dmitri Harkonnen had set up the secret delivery for House Mutelli, which went against strict Imperial laws. The landed cargo cutter should already be loaded with black-market spice. The governor simply could not conceive that the Fremen would strike. A fool! He greatly underestimated them.

Several more grenades leveled an oval administrative shack, and then a handful of Harkonnen guards appeared out of nowhere, armed with . . . stunners? Mapes was surprised the ruthless offworlders would bother with the limited lethality of stunners. Why not just kill the Fremen outright?

Onorio fell when a stunner beam caught his legs and rendered him unable to walk. He thrashed on the sand, still crawling forward to kill more enemies.

Running hard, Mapes reached the open craft on the landing field, saw only one armed man at the boarding ramp. One guard? He drew his stunner, glowered at her, raised the weapon. Without hesitation, she hurled her crysknife, and the blade embedded itself in the base of his throat. As he crumpled to the ramp, clutching at his neck, the guard seemed appalled that he had been beaten so easily. Arrogant, foolish Harkonnens!

Mapes knelt beside his body and withdrew her sacred knife. The milky blade was covered with his blood.

She also drew her Maula pistol, spring-wound and ready, and bounded into the transport, ready to fight anyone else aboard.

Would they wear body shields inside? It didn't matter to her which way the enemy died.

But she found the piloting deck empty, the vessel unoccupied. Where was the delivery crew? The House Mutelli representative?

She prowled forward, uneasy. The ship's cargo area was also empty, not a single package of melange . . . and she had seen no spice out on the landing field for loading. According to what she'd learned in Governor Harkonnen's office, there should have been a significant load. This could not be correct.

With growing alarm, she checked the controls on the piloting deck. The cargo transport seemed functional, ready to depart. She knew this was the night for the scheduled shipment.

Explosions continued out in the base, accompanied by shouts and the sounds of more killing. She ducked back outside to look for Rafir, to shout a caution, although her suspicions were not yet confirmed.

He and his commandos rushed to the spice silos, worked to access the melange stockpile inside. But as Rafir's team opened the hatches, instead of finding a treasure trove of spice, armed fighters boiled out. Harkonnens!

Soldiers lay in wait inside the silos, and now they sprang their trap. Many of them did wear thrumming body shields, which rendered the Fedaykin weapons less effective. They surged out and opened fire with stunners, cutting down the front line of commandos.

Rafir shouted, "Hai ha! Treachery!"

At the hatch of the cargo transport, Mapes absorbed the change in an instant. Had it all been a trick? Did Dmitri Harkonnen intentionally leave the shipment memo exposed for his housekeeper to see? How did he know? Had she herself delivered tainted information that led her comrades into a trap?

"No!" She dashed to the piloting deck, activated the aircraft's systems, and the suspensor engines thrummed as they built to nominal energy levels. She thrust her head out of the open hatch and shouted in Chakobsa so the Harkonnens wouldn't understand. "There is nothing here for us! Run to the transport, and I will fly us away."

At the silos, Rafir fought like a dust devil, his crysknife slashing.

The other Fedaykin tried to save themselves, but the Harkonnens used stunners to mow down four more, leaving them helpless on the ground.

"Keep them alive if you can," barked a Harkonnen officer.

"I'd rather kill all the scum!"

"Aye, they'll be killed, but in a slow Harkonnen way. Governor wants to make an example of them."

Mapes felt a deeper horror. This was not only a trap, but a truly insidious one. The Fedaykin had been lured here for this very purpose. Had Governor Harkonnen recognized Mapes as a spy? Was she at fault? "Run! To the ship! Rafir!"

Two Fedaykin broke away from their Harkonnen opponents and sprinted across the glassy landing field toward the cargo transport, trying to get to her in time, but they were cut down.

All Fremen commandos were taught how to steal and fly ornithopters and other common craft, and Mapes knew she could figure out these somewhat unfamiliar controls. At last she succeeded in raising the craft on its suspensor engines and felt the soft hum around her.

Rafir and Ahar bolted toward the rising transport, and she nudged it closer, maneuvering so they had a chance of climbing aboard. More Harkonnen soldiers appeared from the opposite side of the camp, emerging from hidden redoubts. Soon they would overwhelm her stolen craft, too.

Rafir sprinted closer, and she held the rim of the hatch, steering toward him. The boarding ramp had been withdrawn, but he could still jump aboard. "Quickly, Rafir!" The Harkonnens were closing in, and they would soon overwhelm the craft. "We have to get away now!"

Ahar stumbled after Rafir, but soldiers overpowered him, stunned him. He collapsed, sprawling headlong on the dusty ground. Rafir had nearly reached the open craft when he saw more troops closing in from all sides. He looked back at Mapes, his glance like a slash of a knife, and he stopped. "Go, my love! I will buy you a few more seconds to escape."

"We don't have seconds!" All the other Fedaykin had been stunned, scattered on the ground, still alive but with no muscle control. "Come, Rafir! You and me. Think of our child." It was a desperate ploy, but she knew of nothing else that might move him.

He shook his head. "You will not make it." Instead of leaping aboard, he thrust the hilt of his crysknife into her hand. "Take this! Raise our child to become a fighter among the Fremen."

"No! Come with me!" she cried, but he turned.

"Go now, or all will be lost." He withdrew one last grenade from his pack, pushed the activator, and hurled it into the oncoming troops. When the blast flattened and scattered them, even the ones wearing shields, Rafir laughed and ran forward, pulling out a plasteel knife so he could continue the killing.

Shuddering, Mapes pushed the suspensor engines and lifted the cutter. Below her, Rafir let out a wild howl just as the stunners cut him down. He tried to raise his knife to cut his own throat and keep the Harkonnens from torturing him, but he could not, and just lay there, struggling to regain control of his body.

Mapes sobbed and nudged the accelerators to move the ship away from the base, gaining altitude.

The Fedaykin commandos had lost, but most of them weren't dead, not yet. Not until the torturers got through with them.

Mapes had to get back to the sietch, beg assistance from her mother. Maybe the Fremen could find a way to rescue the prisoners if Governor Harkonnen meant to take them back to Carthag for interrogation . . . or some other public spectacle. She clung to that thin spiderweb of hope and flew the craft away from the base on her way out to the open desert.

An explosion rocked the starboard engine, throwing Mapes from the control panel. She hadn't had time to activate the ship's shields, and someone had launched a rocket to bring down the craft. She had to put other thoughts aside and just keep herself aloft, to fly the damaged vessel as far into the desert as she could. Then she would use her Fremen skills to survive.

The cargo transport would not last long. Fuel was leaking, and one engine was burning. The ungainly craft lumbered along, barely above the ground, and she clipped a rock outcropping that damaged the portside aileron. With no safe destination possible, she pushed the craft out into the vast expanse of sand. She knew she didn't have much time, but every kilometer gave her more of a chance. Mapes was a Fremen. She could live in the rigors of the desert, but the Harkonnens could not.

She managed to stay aloft for four minutes before the craft crunched down against the dunes, clipped, lurched, and rolled. The starboard engine still smoked. Mapes was dazed by the impact, and her forehead bled from a deep cut, but thanks to her metabolism, the blood coagulated quickly.

She scrambled away from the wreckage, plodded and stumbled onto the loose sand. Behind her from the direction of the Sihaya Ridge base, she saw bright lights rise in the sky and streak toward her. *Pursuit craft.* They would be here soon.

The impact of the crash had caused deep vibrations in the desert, and a worm would come soon. She hoped it would engulf the site while the Harkonnens were here looking for her body. The night was her friend, her only hope.

Mapes sprinted away, fleeing for her life and from the terrible reality of what had just happened. She ran with an erratic gait, knowing that she left clear footprints, but the turmoil of a worm would erase them all.

She crossed a dune crest and slid down the slipface. At the bottom she pulled her desert cloak around her and covered herself with sand, then lay in perfect silence, listening to the cacophony of grief inside her mind and heart.

She might never see her beloved Rafir again, might never know his strength or the gentleness of his touch. Their child was in her womb, so now she had to live for both of them.

V

Surviving felt worse than death. If Rafir and the others had been killed in the raid, Mapes would have felt crushed. Knowing they were taken alive made the burden even heavier.

Gloom and anger filled the sietch like the unsettling stench of a faulty reclamation chamber. Naib Safia made an awkward announcement celebrating how much damage the Fedaykin had bought with their blood, but that blood price had not yet been paid. The Fremen understood that Governor Harkonnen's revenge would come at an extraordinarily high cost.

Mapes's heart and mind were a Coriolis storm of grief, disappointment, and shame. She wanted to replay every detail of that night, but in a way that she could recognize the clues and the trap, and warn the Fedaykin in time. The Harkonnens had tricked her; Mapes could not deny it. She was the one who had provided the false information taken from the governor's office. It was her fault.

Mapes now had two crysknives, her own and Rafir's. On impulse, she followed the tunnels and ascended to the speaking alcove. She stood for a long moment in silence, watching the busy sietch activities. When she could no longer hold her anguish inside, she raised both milky blades and called out in her loudest voice, "We cannot wallow in defeat and death. We must go on a raid! We are Fremen!"

The faces turned up to her, their spice-blue eyes staring. Many of the expressions were hurt, some hopeless, others fired with anger. "Our Fedaykin were captured, and they are now held in Carthag. I know the prison! I saw it during my time in the city. Working together, we can free them and flee into the desert." Her voice cracked. "And we will kill many Harkonnens as we do so."

When Mapes heard the lackluster response from the crowd

below, her heart broke. Naib Safia, limping on her prosthetic leg, entered the speaking alcove behind her and placed an arm around her daughter's shoulder, but Mapes did not want maternal comfort. She needed a naib's vengeful leadership.

Safia's low voice nevertheless trickled into the grotto for the tribe to hear. "That is not possible, Daughter. The Harkonnens already hunt us out of spite. If we provoke them further, as you suggest, we would face outright war, and our people would surely lose. Those Fedaykin are already lost to us, whether or not the water has left their bodies."

"But we are Fremen!" Mapes clutched a crysknife in each hand. "This planet is ours."

"Dune is ours, as it has been for thousands of years," Safia said, "and will be for thousands more. Our individual lives are dust grains blown on the wind, but the dunes remain. We Fremen will remain."

"I need to free Rafir," Mapes said in a hoarse voice. Her hand strayed to her abdomen.

"Then try to find another way," her mother said.

MAPES DID AS the naib suggested, remembering that she had other skills, powers beyond an outright attack. She could be small, unobtrusive, invisible. Perhaps that was a better way to free Rafir. At least she could find a way to see him, one last time . . .

Telling no one, not even her mother, she slipped away from the sietch and traveled back to the dirty city of Carthag. Each moment weighed on her because Dmitri Harkonnen was not a patient man. Wanting to make his grim point, he would not delay his revenge for long, but Mapes hoped he would want to savor the building dread among the people he ruled.

Again, she donned a drab household outfit, the same colorless robes she had worn inside the governor's mansion. By claiming to be on an errand for the siridar governor, she obtained a discarded message cylinder and an official-looking document written in a flowery, high-imperial dialect. Actually, it was merely a decree about modifications to waste-distribution systems in the city of Arsunt, but no one would look closely at the words. They would see only the cylinder, the Harkonnen griffin seal, and Mapes's confidence.

As couriers and daily supply deliveries entered the blocky prison, Mapes wove her cloak of psychological invisibility and walked with her head down, message cylinder in hand. At the gates, she mumbled to the thick-necked sentry, "Message from the governor's household. I require access."

The door sentry scowled at her small form and dusty clothes. Mapes made sure that he saw her tremble in fear as she held up the message cylinder as proof. He scrutinized Mapes more than he did the cylinder and then, when several annoyed bureaucrats queued up behind her, he motioned her inside with a jerk of his chin.

Mapes scuttled through the imposing door, moving with mannerisms that proved she knew what she was doing and where she was going. When she located the extensive ranks of prisoner cells, her next challenge was to identify where Rafir, Ahar, Onorio, and the other commandos were held.

The Carthag prison complex was crowded far beyond capacity, chamber after chamber, large cells and small. Mapes was astonished to see how many people had been swept off the streets for imagined infractions.

Whenever someone challenged her in the corridor, Mapes waved the message cylinder and moved past. Seeing so many prisoners awaiting trial, the impossible backlog of harsh justice, Mapes wondered if Governor Harkonnen might simply forget about Rafir and his small band, but when she saw spice-paper posters on the walls announcing the imminent public execution, with images of Rafir and the others, Mapes felt her heart turn to stone.

In the highest-security wing of the prison, the guards were harder, more alert, and Mapes knew she would need finesse to bluff her way to the actual cells. She looked from side-to-side, wondering where she might locate her friends.

A square-faced man stopped her, stepping in front of the small woman to block her way. "You may not proceed. Violent criminals are inside."

"But, m'Lord, I have orders from the governor." She showed him the message cylinder.

The guard's voice sounded like a massive door slamming shut. "You should fear for your safety, a young woman like you, small and weak . . ."

It took all of Mapes's strength not to kill him on the spot. Instead, she averted her eyes and bowed her head. "I am confident that Harkonnen security will keep me safe. I must speak privately with the terrorist prisoners. The governor ordered me to deliver this message."

"Why would he send someone like you?"

"Because," she swallowed, "he wants one of their own people to read them the news. He says it will be more painful that way."

The guard's brow furrowed. "Are you one of those terrorists? You know them?"

She shook her head, kept her eyes down. "No, m'Lord. I am just a poor woman from the town, but my family came from the desert . . . a long time ago. The governor thinks we are all terrorists." She raised her chin. "And we are not."

"Go ahead, then." He turned to follow her. "I want to hear what the governor has to say."

"No, m'Lord! He told me I had to face them alone." She made her voice quaver. "He said that I have to do a good job, or I will join them in execution." When the square-faced guard remained doubtful, she said, "He will ask me for a report, and I must be truthful or he will know. I would have to inform him that you eavesdropped." She looked up, met the guard's eyes for just a second, then remembered to flick them away. "It is your choice, m'Lord. I cannot tell you what to do."

The guard's expression soured, and he nudged her into the prison block. "Fourth cell down the corridor. Go! They're not all conscious, but you can deliver your message to anyone able to hear you." He stepped farther away from the door. "I won't listen. Do not say that I did."

Mapes believed him. She scuttled down the dusty corridor until she reached a force-barred chamber, a crackling static field supplemented by old iron rods.

"Rafir," she said in a low whisper. Inside the confinement, she saw him lurch up from a stone bench. Several other Fedaykin stirred, cautiously moving toward the crackling bars. Some remained defiant, while others had their spirits crushed.

Rafir's dark blue eyes lit up, but with horror rather than hope. "Hai ha! You should not be here! You cannot—"

"I had to come for you." Again, she unconsciously touched her abdomen. "No choice."

He understood, but his demeanor didn't change. "You must get yourself safe. There is nothing you can do here. I cannot let you die with us."

"I will not," she said. "And I will find a way to help you escape." Her voice hitched, and her guilt formed words she could not speak, that she blamed herself for the false information that had caused this disaster. "I can break you free. It is a . . . a spirit demand on me."

"No! It is too dangerous."

She lowered her voice, longing to hold him. "No danger is too great." She wished she could break through the shimmering field and just whisk him away.

Onorio lay motionless on the floor, his head crusted with dark blood. Ahar nursed a broken arm. The other commandos were downcast, having accepted their fates. Now they shook their heads, agreeing with Rafir.

"I swear to you, my love, this is not possible," Rafir said. "Even if our whole sietch came to fight in Carthag, we would all die."

"Then we will die fighting," Mapes said. "I cannot and will not give up."

"You must. We have been captured, and the governor means to make an example of us. From the moment they sprang their trap at Sihaya Ridge, the future was determined. You cannot reverse the wind that has blown." The other Fedaykin did not beg or plead; they simply listened to Rafir, their leader.

"But I escaped! That must have been for a purpose. My life is devoted to seeing you free again."

"Listen to me—this once, even if never again. You are carrying my child. You must devote your life to raising a new Fremen, helping another generation grow strong and fight. I am done." He gestured to his fellow prisoners. "Hai ha, we are all done. Forget about me."

"You still live. I can never forget about you."

Rafir's face became awash with love. "Then make certain our son or daughter grows up to know me. But you have to slip away! Get out of this prison before they discover who you are. Continue to fight."

"I would never stop fighting," Mapes said, "but you cannot ask me to leave. I came to break you out."

He stared at her for a long moment. "You may have told yourself so, my love, but that is not the reason you came. In your heart, you know that you came to say goodbye. I love you so much for that."

Her throat closed, blocking words for a long moment. Finally, she said in a cracked whisper, "Goodbye, my love. You will live forever in my heart."

"And in our child," Rafir said. "Keep the baby safe. Keep yourself safe."

Devastation wrapped around her like a heavy cloak. "I have failed you twice."

"You have made me happier than any man on Dune."

At the far end of the corridor she saw the square-faced guard watching her. He saw the anguish on her face and was satisfied. She turned back to Rafir. "I will be there for you up until the last moment. Governor Harkonnen has announced the time and place of your execution. Know that I will be there."

He recoiled. "No! You will make it worse. I forbid it! Promise me you will not watch. Please . . ."

"But I have to." She reached out, stopped with her fingers a hair's breadth from the pulsing field. "I need to support you in the only way I can."

"Then support me by going away. Remember only our best times. If you watch the execution, then that will be all you can remember."

An animal sound groaned deep in her throat, and she wanted to shrink away and truly become invisible.

"Promise me!" Rafir insisted.

The other Fedaykin came closer. "He is right, Mapes," Ahar said. "Do not watch us. That will only make it worse . . . for everyone."

She could only make a silent promise, unable to utter the words. She turned to flee, clutching the false message cylinder against her. She held onto the image of Rafir's face, her last glimpse of him. She nodded briefly in defeat and hurried away. Seeing her misery, the Harkonnen guard grinned and let her go.

MAPES REMAINED IN Carthag until the day of the execution. She longed to stay and hold up her hands for Rafir. She wanted him to look into her eyes in his last moment of life, let him see *her* rather than death, but she remained true to her word. She would not witness the execution, but she did stay until the prisoners were brought forth.

Trying to be invisible again, Mapes melted into the uneasy crowd as Rafir and the Fedaykin were stripped naked under the hot sun and tied to pillars in the public square. Dmitri Harkonnen had announced that they would all be painted with acid, every inch of their skin, and when the chemical ate away the skin, another layer of acid would be applied, again and again, until nothing remained but bones.

Biting back a scream, Mapes heard the pronouncement, saw the guards step forward with barrels of caustic chemical. They wore protective suits, were ready to perform the horrific task. Mapes silently shrank and screamed, but no one around her noticed. She stared until she knew she had to go.

Turning, she made her way out of the crowd, pushing against the flow of people. She clung to the love she would always feel. She hurried off, wrapping her arms around her belly, vowing to her unborn child that she would never let Rafir be forgotten.

When the screams began behind her, she tried to block her ears, steeled herself and hurried away. The clamor of executions and crowd noises rose in the square, but Mapes did not turn around, remembering her promise.

PART II

10,152 A.G.
Seventeen Years Later

VI

Under glowglobe light in the sietch chamber, the edge of the crysknife gleamed. Mapes wrapped her calloused hand around the worn hilt, felt the grip. The weapon was part of her. She stood on the balls of her feet on the sandy cave floor as she studied the second crysknife held by the shirtless young man. He had death in his eyes as he faced her. His fighting stance was perfect, and she knew he would take advantage of any mistake she made.

But Mapes did not make mistakes. If she had, she would have died long ago.

The young man slashed at her, and she danced back without being touched, smooth as the wind. He pushed closer, stabbing, slashing, but she dodged every blow. Narrowing her gaze, Mapes was alert to the slightest changes in his expression, the flicker or twitch that might give away his next move. Samos was a deft fighter and unpredictable—the best and most dangerous killer.

She brought her blade up, and the polished worm tooth clacked against his knife, razor edge against razor edge. She pressed him back with surprising strength, and he released an outburst of air. Taking advantage, she brought up her other hand and smacked his wrist, knocking the knife away. He let his knees collapse, evading her as she slashed at his face. He dropped backward out of the way, struck the ground with his bare shoulders for no longer than a gnat might touch skin, and sprang up again. Just the way she had taught him to do.

"Good!" As his mother, she was always spare with her praise, because compliments could make a person weak. When Samos grinned, she could see the achingly familiar echoes of his father's rakish smile. How she missed Rafir!

As the sixteen-year-old sprang to his feet, he went into the wary combat stance again. Mapes had never lost her poise.

Sitting in her chair on the side of the chamber, old Naib Safia chuckled. "This could take all day. Those knives cannot be put away unless one is blooded."

Mapes and Samos dueled each other, crysknife against crysknife, her mother's sacred blade in her hand, against Rafir's used so skillfully by their son. "I did not expect this to be swift. I taught my son everything I know."

"Ah, but I am capable of learning new tricks," Samos said, "while my mother is too set in her ways." He switched the blade to his left hand, jabbed the point at her face, and Mapes ducked back, easily avoiding the tip. But the young man used the diversion to fling his legs out and kick her feet, knocking her to the ground. He pounced, and Mapes rolled. She felt the razor edge graze past her cheek, only a whisper away from cutting her skin. . . .

Years ago, after the execution of Rafir and the Fedaykin, Mapes had withdrawn to the sietch, where she'd cared for the growing baby in her womb. When their son was born, she had spent every day fashioning him into a Fremen, teaching him to be a Fedaykin. A hatred for the Harkonnens was burned into every cell of his body.

Over the years, Governor Harkonnen had continued to punish the Fremen, and when he could not locate the wild desert tribes, he took out his ire on the townspeople, the dusty traders, the poor dwellers of the pan and graben. The Harkonnens did not know the difference among the desert people, nor did they care. Oppression was its own reward.

Mapes had never stopped plotting to kill Dmitri Harkonnen, and she had raised her boy with that singular purpose as well. Unfortunately, when Samos was only a boy of ten, Dmitri Harkonnen was assassinated on Giedi Prime, killed far out of her reach, for reasons entirely unrelated to any Fremen revenge. Mapes felt cheated, though she was glad to know the loathsome man was dead.

Thus, she decided to raise Samos to kill other Harkonnens, never to forget their mission to drive the offworlders from Dune. For the past six years, Abulurd Harkonnen, the son of Dmitri, had served as siridar governor here, a lackluster man who nevertheless must be evil by his very existence. Samos would have someone to kill.

Now her energetic son sprang at her again, his head ducked low as if he meant to butt her in the stomach, but his crysknife was raised high. She bent her back out of the way, then slashed as he went past. She did not pull her strike, didn't hesitate in any way. Nor did Samos. She had taught the young man that there was no such thing as a practice duel. Every fight was to the death. If he was good enough to spar with her, then he was good enough to fight with all of his blood and energy.

Naib Safia watched and laughed. "You have made him into a good fighter, Mapes. But he needs to be resilient enough to fight Harkonnens."

Mapes and Samos did not take their eyes from each other, watching for any flinch in their opponent. But while they were so intently focused, Safia hurled her prosthetic leg in between them. Samos nearly tripped on the sudden obstacle, while Mapes leaped over it. Her mother crowed, "A real fight isn't always a tidy little duel!"

Bounding back, Samos thrust at Mapes. She caught his crysknife, slid it away, then slashed. His knife was a blur, and she parried, both of them using each hand, kicking out with their feet. She extended her reach just a bit, stretched enough to cut, and felt the milky blade nick his skin. She darted back, raising her crysknife and calling an end to the fight. She saw a spot of dark red welling on his bare chest.

"Blood!" she said. "A magnificent fight, but I have drawn first blood."

Instead of looking defeated, Samos grinned. "Look at your arm, mother." She saw a tiny scratch on her skin, blood already congealing. She had not even felt the cut. Satisfied, she sheathed her crysknife. "All is proper."

Samos was flushed, overheated, and he calmed himself. "When I fight Harkonnens, Mother, I will leave more than a scratch."

VII

I see a weakness in this Abulurd Harkonnen," said Naib Safia as she sat at a low table inside her private chamber. The two women sipped spice coffee, ate honeyed wafers, and plotted death and destruction.

"He is softer than his half-brother Vladimir," Mapes agreed. "He even considers himself compassionate, wants the people to view him as a good ruler."

"That is his failing." Her mother took a long sip of steaming coffee. "What matters is whether or not the Padishah Emperor considers him a good governor. That man measures only the spice profits the throne can take from Dune."

"Even with so many Harkonnens killed?" Mapes asked. "Does no one notice the losses?" She finished her honey wafer and touched her fingertips together. The golden substance was tacky like drying blood.

The Fedaykin raids had continued, even increased since Abulurd became governor. Samos and several friends had formed a vicious and successful group of commandos, seizing any opportunity to strike, injure, and kill. Her son had even recruited two young women—like his mother, and her mother before her—into his ruthless fighters. He reserved his only passion to avenge his father's murder, which made Mapes both proud and sad, because even Rafir had found time for tenderness with her. When she questioned her son about the possibility of love, Samos had responded that he would become tender when Dune was free.

"Emperor Elrood does not care how many Harkonnen soldiers are killed." Safia snorted, taking another wafer. "I doubt the governor even reports those losses to Kaitain. It would be considered an internal matter."

Mapes nodded. "Thus, my point. Simply attacking guard stations and cutting Harkonnen throats does not help our cause . . . though it brings its own satisfaction. We need to attack the spice operations, and hit hard enough so that the Emperor notices. We must drive out Abulurd Harkonnen the same way you drove out House Richese, Mother."

The following afternoon, Samos and his ragged commandos returned exhausted and bloodied, overjoyed but also griefstruck. Mapes pushed through the crowds of tense onlookers, relieved to see her son alive. His face was bruised from a fight, and his gaze was downcast. Some of the Fedaykin were cheering, while others remained quiet and sullen.

"How many did we lose?" Mapes barked. Behind her, Naib Safia hobbled on her artificial leg.

"Two." Samos lifted his chin. "We brought down one of their patrol 'thopters. Four of us were walking out on the open dunes, intentionally exposed in the daylight. As soon as we heard the 'thopter approach, the rest of the team prepared the ambush. It worked." He ground his jaw, looked at her. "It worked, Mother!"

"If two of our people died, then it did not work entirely."

"But we slew six of them, and we captured their 'thopter. They landed, intending to kill us, but Fremen are not so easy to kill." Mutters of agreement rippled up from the crowd. "We lay in wait, and sprang our trap. We killed them cleanly, then flew their craft back here to the sietch."

Naib Safia nodded. "Now we have another 'thopter."

"Two Fremen are dead," Mapes pointed out, thinking of Rafir and his executed companions.

"And so are six Harkonnens," her son insisted. "Their bodies are already in the reclamation stills. Their water belongs to the tribe."

Mapes was upset, but she realized that most of her anger and frustration was out of concern for Samos, and she needed to put that aside. He was doing the work that she herself had done and would continue to do. Rafir had been the same way, and he had paid the ultimate price. There would always be a cost and a risk, and as long as the cost to the Harkonnens was greater, the Fremen were achieving their goals.

"Yes, their water belongs to the tribe." Mapes reached up to embrace her son.

Two days later when the Huanui deathstills had extracted every drop of moisture from the Harkonnen bodies, Samos reverently brought his mother an ornate chalice that had been stolen from a Richesian government building years ago. He offered it to her. "The water of our enemies, Mother."

She looked at the cool, clear liquid and took a sip. "Harkonnen water. It has a bitter taste."

She gave the goblet back to Samos, who took a longer gulp. "I disagree. To me, it tastes sweet."

VIII

Slipping into the Arrakeen Residency proved to be less of a challenge than infiltrating Dmitri Harkonnen's administrative mansion in Carthag. The former governor had been hard, paranoid, and careful, but his son was not nearly afraid enough. The Harkonnen family name struck fear among the people, but Mapes was not easily frightened. She had mastered the art of looking timid and cooperative, drawing no notice as she did her duties and accomplished her own aims.

Abulurd had been raised on the industrial world of Giedi Prime and served as the steward of the cold, wet planet of Lankiveil. He was a thin man with shaggy ash-blond hair and large expressive eyes. His generous lips and widow's peak reminded Mapes of Dmitri Harkonnen, but Abulurd did not seem to have broken glass inside him, as his father did.

Instead of Carthag, with its square buildings, metal walls, and crowded barracks, the older city of Arrakeen and its more ornate Residency had better suited Abulurd when he came here to accept his role. He felt the old building had character and majesty, even though his construction crews were taking more than six years to complete the modifications he desired. Abulurd seemed to be a different sort of governor, though. He increased rations and pay among the household staff, and when a year went by without capricious executions, the quivering undertone of fear began to fade. Mapes did not believe it.

She once again found a place among the Residency staff, performing her work and silently observing, looking for some advantage she could use. The new governor's iron grip might have been looser than his father's, but the staff let their own corruption grow rampant behind the scenes. To Mapes, those self-serving people were like wanderers without a paracompass, while she had a singular drive: ruining the siridar governor so that Emperor Elrood IX would whisk him away.

Though she acknowledged the satisfaction of spilled blood from enemies she had slain, Mapes grew more impressed with what she could quietly do as an invisible housekeeper, someone who had unnoticed access to numbers, orders, and schedules. Back at the sietch, she had spent a great deal of time learning the machinery of administration, understanding the records kept by the governor, the garrison, and the spaceport.

By altering dates or quantities on a manifest, by diverting deliveries or spreading out patrol assignments, she could cause as much damage as a commando raid.

Exactly as her mother had taught her, Mapes let her coworkers underestimate her. The Harkonnens regarded the dirty townspeople as poor, ignorant, even illiterate, but Mapes knew that the downtrodden people moved sluggishly not out of incompetence, but through quiet, resolute resistance.

In the Arrakeen Residency, Mapes served meals, cleaned rooms, worked the laundry. She took advantage of any time she could be alone in Governor Abulurd's offices. Though he had numerous administrators, the man liked to perform work himself, claiming that it gave a personal touch. He claimed that a good governor should be aware of his supply chain, his troop lodgings and all their assignments. Abulurd wanted to know all the incoming ships that delivered equipment and necessary materiel to the Arrakis operations.

Without his knowledge, Mapes found those records, searched manifests, looked at schedules and delivery instructions. With a smile, she changed a field on the official forms and modified delivery instructions. In that one quick action she caused more damage than a hundred Fedaykin grenades.

The large shipment of water and packaged food was destined for Harkonnen troops in the Arrakeen barracks. With over a hundred thousand troops stationed in Arrakeen, Carthag, and a dozen outposts around the Shield Wall, these supplies were a lifeline paid for by House Harkonnen supplemented by an Imperial stipend.

Mapes had changed the offloading instructions and the delivery date, and she made sure to arrange for local cargo handlers as soon as the shipment landed, city dwellers who were not beholden to Harkonnens—and it all arrived a day earlier than Governor Abulurd's records indicated.

When the ship landed, full of bounty, the captain and crew followed the modified instructions on the manifest, delivering the water, food, clothing, tools, and equipment to the poor and starving people of Arrakeen. Everything was distributed in a flash.

Mapes wanted to be there at the spaceport to witness her malicious largesse, but her greater revenge was to remain in the Residency and watch as the news came in. She quietly cleaned in the office wing, listening but unobtrusive. Rags covered her head and shoulders.

An alarmed guard rushed in to report to Abulurd. "Governor, the supply shipment landed, but everything is gone, confiscated by the people. The delivery went to the wrong place. They are a mob."

"Shipment?" Abulurd sounded perplexed rather than alarmed. "I just reviewed the schedule this morning. It arrives tomorrow. Our supplies are not due until then."

"It is here, sir! Everything is taken. The water, the food. It's all gone."

Abulurd blinked. "Well then, we must get it back. The people will have to surrender them. Those supplies rightfully belong to the Harkonnen troops stationed here."

The soldier shook his head. "The captain showed us the manifest. It appears to be legitimate."

Abulurd frowned down at the report printed on spice paper. "This must be some mistake. Yes, yes it is clearly an error. Send our apologies to the people, but we must have the water back."

The soldier remained aghast. "But . . . m'Lord, it is gone. The water has been divided among thousands. The people have whisked away the food. We will never find it again unless you mean to uproot every home, ransack each room, interrogate the families."

Abulurd recoiled. "That would cause terrible unrest. Such a setback." He sat at the large bloodwood desk that had once belonged to his father. "I shall write my half-brother on Giedi Prime and request a replacement shipment." He clucked his tongue against his teeth. "Vladimir will not like the additional cost, but perhaps we can make up for it with a few months of extra spice production." He nodded to himself. "Yes, the people received an unexpected wind-fall, and all that food and water should keep them happy. Thus, they will work harder, produce more."

Mapes listened in the corridor, scowling. The governor did not understand the people here at all. Their windfall came from in-competence or intentional sabotage, and she would help spread the word as to exactly what had happened. They would not respond with increased loyalty, would not work harder, would not produce a single extra grain of spice. How could Abulurd possibly weather the storm of his violent brother's anger? Replacing the supply shipment would cost the Harkonnen treasury a fortune, just as Mapes had intended.

It would certainly be noticed in the Imperial court.

If she could disgrace Abulurd in the eyes of the Emperor, leave the valuable spice-harvesting operations in disarray and financially unfeasible, then the siridar governor would soon be gone. What she had done was an excellent step in the right direction.

IX

For the seven years Abulurd Harkonnen served as governor of Arrakis, the Fremen continued to harry, attack, and embarrass him. Trying his best, he increased security and took punitive actions, but his attitude was more consternation than fury. With each setback, his position eroded further.

With the sage advice of Naib Safia and the deliberative planning of Mapes, the commandos repeatedly hit and hurt the spice operations. For the most part, Governor Abulurd managed to cover the accidents and shortfalls with loans from the Harkonnen treasury. Mapes imagined that his half-brother on Giedi Prime must be enraged at such incompetence.

"Our only true victory will come when Emperor Elrood feels the pain like a deep wound," said Safia as she addressed a group of Fremen elders and Fedaykin.

"We have damaged their equipment, ruined spice harvesters, sabotaged shipments," Mapes pointed out, "Melange production under Abulurd Harkonnen is markedly down, and the Emperor knows it."

Her son, Samos, the youngest man in the meeting, spoke up with a fiery voice. "Numbers on a report may be damning, but we must do something that will be noticed, a crippling blow rather than an embarrassment! Spice is the only weapon we can use. We can no longer whittle away at these offworlders bit by bit. We can't just nick them with the tip of a crysknife. We must deal a mortal wound."

The Fremen around the convocation table muttered and nodded as if they all understood, but Mapes let out an impatient sigh. "A bold statement, Samos, but that means nothing without a bold plan—a specific plan followed by specific action."

The young man's wolfish grin reminded her so much of Rafir's.

"And that is exactly what I have in mind, Mother." He unrolled a long sheet of spice paper that held a detailed topographical map of a section of the Shield Wall far south of Arrakeen. He pointed out a small, clear basin surrounded by rugged terrain, high cliffs. "This is the Orgiz refinery complex, one of the largest melange-processing facilities on Dune. It has been in operation for two hundred years, but Dmitri Harkonnen expanded it, fortified it. Fully twenty percent of the spice processed and shipped each month passes through there."

"We know this, young Samos," said the naib. "It is a golden target, but unattainable. Hundreds of heavily armed Harkonnen troops are stationed there, with fortifications, even shields. The walls and barricades are high. With their weaponry and entrenched defensive position, it would take thousands of Fedaykin even to have a chance."

Mapes shook her head. "Even then, it would be a slaughter on both sides."

Her son brightened. "I propose to use a weapon stronger than anything the Harkonnens possess."

"And what kind of weapon is that?" Mapes pulled out her sheathed crysknife and set it on the table, and Samos also removed his, the one that had belonged to his father, resting it alongside hers.

He bent over the detailed map again. "The Orgiz complex is shielded by high volcanic mountains, where it is protected from storms and the open desert. But look here." He traced his finger along a winding narrow canyon, following the crack on the topographic map, until he demonstrated where it widened and opened out to the desert, though it was all but hidden. "Look, they have a vulnerability, a back door."

Naib Safia studied the route. "You intend to bring Fedaykin in there? They will be vulnerable in that narrow defile."

"Not just Fedaykin. Something that even a Harkonnen army cannot withstand." He paused, waiting for them.

Mapes realized what he meant. "A worm! We can drive a worm in there!"

He nodded. "No wild worm would ever find its way into the fortified basin through that convoluted canyon, but Fremen can drive it in. Our wormriders can guide Shai-Hulud like a battering ram. No Harkonnen weapon could stop it, and their shields would drive it mad!"

Naib Safia laughed out loud. The other Fremen in the chamber muttered, their voices rising in excitement.

"A rampaging worm would destroy the major spice operations, and Governor Abulurd could not even blame us," Mapes said, then turned to her son. "I approve of your plan, on one condition—I must accompany your team. We do this together." She knew Rafir would approve.

She looked at Safia, and the old naib nodded her consent.

THE HISS OF sand beneath the huge worm sounded angry, a challenge. Twelve Fedaykin rode on the rough ridged back, and Samos had lashed himself to the topmost ridge where he used goads to drive the worm along the edge of the rugged Shield Wall. Samos knew the secret crack, the long and winding defile that would allow the worm to enter and cause mayhem.

Farther down the long sinuous body, also lashed in place with hooks and ropes, Fedaykin used spreaders to pry open gaps between worm segments, exposing tender flesh so that the creature remained out of the sand rather than burrowing deep. Samos guided it along . . . a weapon that the Harkonnens could not even imagine.

To minimize their chance of being spotted in the open desert, the Fedaykin had made their move just as darkness fell. The group of commandos had headed out, set up a base camp in the rocks, and waited for their firebrand leader. Wearing a desert-camouflaged cloak to keep him invisible in the sand and rocks, Samos had scouted up the narrow canyon that twisted and turned, a mere gash in the mountains. No casual observer would have deemed it anything other than a blind end, but Samos verified that it was wide enough for a worm, and that was all the commandos needed to know.

When they were ready, the Fremen placed a thumper in the sands just outside of the hidden canyon mouth, then wound and released the clockwork mechanism so that the steady, rhythmic pounding would call a worm.

The Fedaykin took their positions, watched the ripple of sand that signaled an oncoming worm, and when the enormous creature rose up to swallow the thumper, the commandos swarmed up its side using spiked boots, hooks, and spreaders to climb and control the worm. With the force of an unstoppable storm, the creature carved through the dunes toward the gap in the wall. "Haiiiii-Yoh!" Samos yelled.

Riding high, Mapes looked at her son, and her heart warmed to see the sixteen-year-old standing on top of the great worm. She could imagine Rafir doing this. *A Fremen weapon, a truly Fremen weapon.* The Harkonnens would know that soon enough.

The worm was reluctant to enter the confined canyon, intractable, knowing it could not turn around in the narrow confines, but Samos used his goads, and other commandos jabbed the soft pink flesh between the rings. Finally, the worm lurched headlong into the canyon, where it had nowhere to go but ahead. The walls rose high and inky with night shadows on either side, and Mapes knew the worm could never retreat. Instead, it was funneled toward its target.

Samos had memorized the path and needed no topographic maps. He diverted the worm away from dead-end side canyons, forcing it deeper and deeper toward the protected basin with the Orgiz refinery.

"The worm will do all the destruction for us!" Mapes shouted to her companions. She felt the exhilaration, feeling young again.

He stood with his spiked boots planted on the rough skin, held onto his ropes, and grinned at her. "I believe you, Mother, but I hope we also find some Harkonnens to kill ourselves. Shai-Hulud cannot have all the fun!"

The canyon walls raced by as the sandworm hurtled toward its destination. Even with the rock walls close on either side, Mapes saw a pale glow ahead in the night, the shimmering haze of lights from the spice-refinery complex. The Fremen cheered, tense and bloodthirsty.

Mapes couldn't tell if the sandworm triggered any proximity alarms as it surged forward, if the Harkonnens had even guarded this obscure perimeter. Did they even know their vulnerability? Given their demonstrated arrogance, she wondered if they had even bothered to explore the maze of side canyons. But after the devastating trap at the Sihaya Ridge base seventeen years earlier, she took nothing for granted.

The lava-rock walls dropped away with startling abruptness to reveal the dazzling compound. It was like an industrial city tucked into the haven of rocks, a basin surrounded by seemingly impregnable mountains. A flat section of the basin floor had been paved to serve as a landing field for carryalls depositing loads of spice. Hangar-sized warehouses and yawning silos stood ready to receive melange shipments delivered from spice factories out in the dunes.

In a glance as swift as a flash of static lightning, Mapes absorbed the details of the processing site, saw the numerous barracks, hundreds of soldiers on patrol, shields, scan-scrambling transmitters. Mapes may have regarded Abulurd Harkonnen as soft and lax, but in this instance he had maintained the strong posture his father had implemented for this huge spice-processing facility. Orgiz was a military fortress protecting giant stockpiles of melange harvested from the sands.

But even a Harkonnen army could not stand against a great worm.

The sinuous beast plunged inside the boxed basin, free of the confining canyon walls. The sandworm thrashed from side-to-side and instinctively targeted the thrumming machinery, the countless Harkonnen troops trapped inside what had become a death cell. The Fremen commandos could barely hold on.

Knowing it was time to dismount, Mapes unlashed the ropes. "Slide down! We will mop up whatever victims Shai-Hulud leaves for us to kill."

Though unable to conceive what was happening, the Harkonnens sounded an alarm, and shrieking sirens ricocheted off the high rock walls. This was like no attack they had ever faced.

Standing on the worm's head like a conquering king, Samos released a wordless shout into the night.

But the Harkonnens thought like offworlders, without regard to the special dangers of the desert, and they responded to the attack in a way that seemed obvious to them. They activated the facility's shields.

Thrumming, flickering barriers appeared around the vulnerable equipment, the spice refineries, the carryalls. The Harkonnen guards also activated personal shields to block any fast-moving projectile fired by a conventional opponent.

But shields drove sandworms into a frenzy.

Sliding down the rough rings of the monster, Mapes had nearly reached the churned ground when the worm writhed as if explosions had gone off throughout its ganglia. Already rampaging into the confined refinery complex, the beast smashed itself against the rock walls, slamming harder and harder.

With well-honed reflexes, Mapes launched herself away, struck the sand, and rolled, trying to get to the shelter of boulders. Above her, she saw several Fedaykin thrown off the worm like debris in a storm.

Perched on the worm's head, Samos struggled to hold his ropes, but the worm was beyond control. The shields drove it into a frenzy. The creature plunged forward, hammered into the rock walls, then dove deep into the sand before bursting up again like a projectile from a gun. Samos was gone in a blur, battered and then scraped away, as unnoticed as a biting fly.

Mapes's scream was lost amid the uproar. The enraged worm rolled and crashed into the refinery operations, slamming itself recklessly into any obstacle, wrecking the carryalls on the landing field despite their protective shields.

She huddled by the boulders at the canyon wall, called out her son's name, but knew she would receive no response. The Orgiz refinery looked as if it were in the midst of a Coriolis storm. The Harkonnen soldiers were entirely impotent against such a monster, even though hundreds rushed out with whatever weapons they possessed. Every one of the Fedaykin was either crushed or buried in the worm's mayhem.

The creature tore through the complex, smashing every building, every craft, every tower. The smell of melange and blood filled the air, cinnamon and iron. Enough spice had been destroyed this night to buy a planet or two, Mapes supposed, but her son was dead.

Shaking, she climbed the rocks, finding handholds that took her up and away from the catastrophe. She had to follow the canyon for a long, long way out into the desert again.

X

Back in Arrakeen, Mapes no longer had to pretend a quiet, dull disinterest in life. She felt numb, but she still had more work to do.

At the Residency, she worked her way into the household staff again so she could watch over Abulurd Harkonnen. Even though some of the workers remembered her from before, they didn't ask questions about where she had gone or why she had returned. Either they supported her efforts to oust Abulurd as governor, or they were afraid to take much interest. Mapes didn't care, one way or the other. She had her own mission.

She knew she should have cherished her victory. The Orgiz refinery had been destroyed, with every single Harkonnen killed. Trapped inside the high-walled basin, the raging worm was unable to find its way back out through the subtle side canyon. For many days, the great creature had battered itself against the high rock walls and attacked any Harkonnen follow-up patrols that swooped in to salvage anything that remained.

Abandoning the entire site, Governor Abulurd Harkonnen signed a notice declaring the Orgiz refinery defunct and assigning all further melange operations to alternate facilities. The setback would resound for years, if not decades, and his shame and embarrassment was absolute. A fifth of the planet's ability to export spice had been erased, and no Harkonnen cover up could hide that from the astute glare of Emperor Elrood.

As she worked in the Arrakeen Residency, Mapes listened to the whispered gossip and the official reports. As a nondescript housekeeper, she remained unnoticed, and even as she mourned her lost son, Mapes kindled the small flame within her. For the past seven years, her purpose had been to overthrow and remove Abulurd Harkonnen. Now she was on the verge of achieving that goal.

The governor walked through the Residency a broken man. His eyes were red rimmed, his face gaunt, his ash-blond hair disheveled, but he tried to display good cheer even with his abysmal disgrace.

After years of lackluster performance, poor spice production, and unforgivable losses, Abulurd's incompetence was plain to the Padishah Emperor. Elrood summarily removed him from his governorship, granting him only enough time to pack a few personal possessions before a private transport would take him to a Guild Heighliner and away from Arrakis.

Mapes managed to scan the official orders and also read the volatile communique from his half-brother, Vladimir. Abulurd would not only be removed from Arrakis, but he would be denied secondary oversight of Giedi Prime, the Harkonnen homeworld. Instead, Abulurd would be swept under the rug to his small out-of-the way holding called Lankiveil, a world of limited natural resources, where he would require little guidance.

On schedule, the enormous Heighliner appeared in orbit over the desert planet, loaded with vessels, cargo haulers, and supplies. At the perimeter of the Arrakeen spaceport, working her way through the spectators, Mapes managed to watch as the hated Abulurd Harkonnen boarded the small lighter that would take him away. The departing governor stood at the boarding ramp, where he turned to look one last time upon his city and the crowds. He raised his hand in farewell, but the dejected people merely grumbled and muttered. No one mourned his departure. When Abulurd realized this, he appeared even more broken, a man with a dead-end future.

The governor's replacement was arriving on the same Heighliner and would take his own transport down to the surface, but Vladimir Harkonnen had expressed his very specific wish that he not be there to watch Abulurd depart. He had no interest in seeing his disgraced brother, who had brought such shame to his noble house.

As the lighter rose into the air, taking Abulurd away, Mapes followed its trajectory until the craft was no more than a silver spark against the dusty yellow skies. She knew the next ship was already inbound from orbit.

Even so, she removed her nose plugs, closed her eyes, and breathed the cracking dry air, smelled the baking heat and the odors of so many unwashed people who stood together. She imagined a new feeling, something that had not been there on Dune for all of her life. For just this brief moment, her world did not have an offworld governor. For just this moment, they were free. Mapes savored the thought.

Before long, a heavy and ornate space yacht landed on the Arrakeen spaceport field, a vessel that boldly displayed the blue griffin of House Harkonnen. Its suspensor engines glowed and a hiss of exhaust curled out an oily black plume.

Mapes felt inexplicably uneasy, but she forced herself to concentrate on her victory, because it had cost her so much . . . Rafir, Samos, all her Fedaykin friends. They had driven out Abulurd Harkonnen, at last.

The private spacecraft opened, and a boarding ramp extended. An escort guard of grim soldiers marched out in perfect formation, weapons raised. They stood to one side, staring ahead. An orange banner unfurled.

Thanks to the constant harassment of Fremen raids, House Richese was gone. Dmitri Harkonnen was gone. And now the incompetent buffoon Abulurd Harkonnen was also gone. This new planetary governor could not possibly be worse.

An immense man emerged from the interior of the space yacht. He wore a cape and a black leather fitted suit of armor that enhanced his muscular body. The shimmer of a personal shield softened his features. He lifted his chin, and his gaze swept like a vulture's across the crowd.

"I am Baron Vladimir Harkonnen," he said in a booming basso voice, "and this planet is mine."

BLOOD
OF THE
SARDAUKAR

The fires of battle had already begun in the city of Arrakeen, shattering a quiet and secure night.

He had a name, but his identity was the uniform and the brotherhood of the Sardaukar, the undefeated elite troops of Emperor Shaddam IV, though now the uniform was false, with loyalties obscured. And Colonel Bashar Jopati Kolona wasn't so sure of his core identity—not on this night, not on this mission. But he had his orders, and he was a Sardaukar.

Arrakeen was the largest city on the desert planet of Arrakis, the seat of House Atreides, newly installed planetary governors in charge of vital spice production for the Imperium. It was also a trap.

Jopati rode inside one of many heavily armored dropships that emerged from an enormous Guild Heighliner in orbit, part of the clandestine Harkonnen attack force augmented by the Imperial military.

On their way down, he saw the aerial bombardment of Arrakeen's slums and warehouses, sparking the first waves of chaos and disrupting Atreides defenses. Low, weathered buildings exploded into dust and flames. When the troop carrier landed hard among the fresh rubble, side doors opened to disgorge the uniformed troops. The colonel bashar led his men, disembarking in a fluid, coordinated motion.

Racing into the streets, the disguised Sardaukar carried projectile weapons and explosive launchers because the Harkonnens liked to kill mass numbers of people from a distance, but Jopati and his troops also carried bladed weapons because they preferred more intimate combat.

He ran ahead through the streets, raising his black-gloved hand.

"Eliminate any resistance, but don't get distracted. Our objective is the Residency, and Duke Leto Atreides will mount a significant defense."

One of the gray-uniformed men beside him snorted. He was not even breathing heavily as they dodged around a broken-down groundcar. "Waste of time."

"Just another day," said a second man, shifting his projectile rifle to aim into the shadows of a narrow alley, where Jopati saw only huddled figures there. No threat.

He said in a stern voice, "Confidence is good, but don't underestimate this Atreides Duke." He smelled the chemical smoke whirling up from the bomb blasts. The air was so brittle and dry here, each breath felt as if it held scouring shards of sand.

Arrakis was a hellish place. Offworlders who worked here by choice could command ridiculously high wages, while other inhabitants were stuck here because they had no place else to go or no way off planet. Jopati had no patience for their whining complaints. This desert world could not compare to the blasted wasteland of Salusa Secundus, the Imperial prison planet the Sardaukar claimed as their home.

Ahead, the great blocky building of the Arrakeen Residency looked more like an illuminated, huddled fortress than the palatial home of a wealthy planetary governor. The walls were thick and square, and the grim architecture reflected decades of Harkonnen rule on Arrakis. Baron Harkonnen and his predecessors were not known for their appreciation of beauty nor their patronage of the arts.

The well-lit Residency stood not far from the Shield Wall, the towering cliffs that protected the city from the dangers of the open desert. The perimeter lights flickered, and more beacons went on as alarms sounded. Atreides guards were already trying to shore up their defenses after the first explosions from the dropships.

The colonel bashar knew his foes could not stand against this well-coordinated sneak attack. The Landsraad might howl and dispute the treacherous actions of the Baron, but Jopati knew full well the accepted treacheries of Imperial politics. He had lived through it himself. The Emperor's role in this overthrow would be covered up, and any hint of Sardaukar participation would be erased. The Landsraad members who objected too strenuously to the treatment of their beloved Duke Atreides would be paid off or, if necessary, assassinated.

Given the sheer number of deadly troops rushing through the city, the outcome of the assault was certain—two legions of Sardaukar descending on the desert planet—one full legion of ten brigades sweeping through Arrakeen itself, and the second legion dispersed to Carthag and other cities around the desert world. They would swiftly remove any Atreides resistance and install Harkonnen-friendly administrators and military peacekeepers.

As his men approached the Residency, launching explosives to disrupt any organized defense, Jopati resented being forced to wear these Harkonnen uniforms, but to his trained eye he could see the difference in how his troops moved, because their service to the Imperium made them better than any other soldier, better than any other human. They were the elite, feared Sardaukar, ferociously loyal to the Padishah Emperor, as bonded to the Imperial throne as a Suk doctor with unbreakable Imperial conditioning. No false uniform could hide that fact from any astute observer.

The lieutenant next to him touched the comm in his ear and grinned. "The house shields are down, Colonel Bashar. Our traitor did his work."

"Acknowledged. We can move right in." Jopati placed his hand on his kindjal, his fighting knife. He was itching to confront the Atreides guards. "Kill anyone necessary, but we have special orders regarding the Duke."

"The Baron will want him himself," said the lieutenant.

"He will, and he's likely to have him," Jopati answered. "But the Emperor gave me explicit orders that Duke Leto is to die cleanly and without torture. I'm to see to it personally. With the enmity these Great Houses feel for one another, the Baron may have . . . difficulty obeying those instructions."

Baron Vladimir Harkonnen was loathsome, not just because of his gross obesity but his carnal, pedophilic appetites, his vicious personality, his utter lack of honor. Thinking of the Baron made Jopati feel dirty in his Harkonnen uniform. He did not care about the politics of Arrakis, or the monopoly on spice production, or the disgusting nature of the Baron himself.

As they ran toward the Residency's main gates, he saw a line of Atreides guards rallying for the fight. Jopati's Sardaukar let out a great roar of challenge and swarmed ahead as explosions continued throughout the city.

At one time, the Atreides Duke was the only person he hated more than the Baron. Now he wasn't so sure.

ALMOST TWO DECADES ago, Jopati Kolona had been on the other side of the same situation. When he was only fourteen, his noble family, House Kolona, were the victims of Landsraad betrayal, a power play by Duke Paulus Atreides—Leto's father—to increase the prominence and profits of House Atreides.

Jopati was the son of Count and Countess Kolona, hereditary rulers of the planet Borhees. He was one of eight sons, five older and two younger. House Kolona had been a member of the Landsraad, faithful if unremarkable citizens of the Imperium for more than a millennium. Borhees was a small planet with a tolerable climate, wealthy enough to be desirable but not enough to be powerful.

In his early teens, Jopati had already known the map of his future, how he would one day become a regional administrator for his Great House, a man who needed to understand bureaucracy and leadership, but who never expected to face many challenges.

That all changed when Count Kolona argued with Duke Paulus Atreides during a Landsraad council session. It was after Imperial laws were changed—conveniently and coincidentally, it seemed—to place House Kolona at a disadvantage, and Paulus pounced on the opportunity for himself. At the council session, Jopati's father filed an appeal and waited for the slow judiciary to grind its way toward a decision.

No one had expected the outright attack from House Atreides.

The warships and nighttime raid had been a complete surprise, and the Kolona house shields had not been activated. Jopati's mother and oldest brother were killed before they even knew what was happening, having gone out to stargaze on an open tower.

A stray explosion struck the rooftop, killing the Countess and the heir. Unprepared for a fight, the Count rallied the rest of his family and whisked them into the hills with little more than the clothes on their backs. All the while the household guards battled the Atreides invaders, giving the Count and his surviving sons time to escape.

Jopati's father had looked sick, angry, and determined. "We will fight one day," he assured the boys as they fled through back passageways. "But it will be a long struggle, and we are not yet ready for battle."

Before that, Jopati had only known peace. Any conflicts were political, such as arguments on the floor of the Landsraad Hall or local Borhees disputes among fur farmers and spider weavers. Before the Atreides Aggression, as his father called it, the greatest emergencies the teenage boy had seen were an unseasonable ice storm that caused widespread damage, and floods that wiped out river villages. In his youth, Jopati had never fought in actual combat, though he had been trained in fencing and hand-to-hand shield fighting—more like a court dance than a clash for survival. Naïve and oblivious, Jopati had been too young to see the real threat posed by Duke Atreides, until the infamous sneak attack.

After that, when the Count led them to his hiding place in the hills, Jopati was astonished to see just how prepared his father actually was. Years before the attack, he had constructed hidden redoubts in sheltered areas and supplied them with weapons and food. Jopati's older brothers knew about the redoubts before he did and had drilled for the unlikely eventuality of an attack, but the teenager had been considered too immature for that information.

Now, after years of harsh training and vigorous military service ingrained in his bones, Colonel Bashar Jopati was deeply disappointed at his father for not establishing more palace defenses and not preparing for a frontal attack. The Sardaukar officer found it ironic that the Atreides themselves were now facing a similar nighttime surprise attack. . . .

For many months the survivors of House Kolona hid in the hills and launched regular guerilla attacks to drive out the Atreides forces that had planted their green-and-black banner on Borhees. Duke Paulus administered the world in the name of Emperor Elrood IX, but he rarely set foot on his new holding. Through intermediaries, Count Kolona continued to file complaints in the Landsraad, and the resistance managed to gain some support, more out of sympathy and vengeance for the murdered Countess and their eldest son than out of any wishful thinking for the golden days of House Kolona. Under occupation, the people of Borhees noticed very little change in their daily lives.

Jopati himself went out on a few guerrilla raids against the Atreides oppressors, which seemed like adventures to him. Inside the protected redoubt, his father continued to spit poison and hatred toward the treacherous Duke Paulus.

After months of hit-and-run harassment, the Duke—or was it the Emperor?—reached a breaking point. The hiding places in the hills were discovered through a spy or a traitor. Military troops swarmed into the hidden redoubt, ruthless fighters wearing the familiar but hated Atreides uniforms. They blasted the sealed entrances and ferreted out the weapons stashes, lookout posts, and satellite command centers. The Kolona guerilla fighters had no chance.

The men in Atreides uniforms were the most efficient and brutal soldiers Jopati had ever seen up to that time in his life. They showed no mercy. With a sweep of his sword, one man beheaded the Count before he could even activate his shield belt. Jopati's four older brothers were also killed before his eyes. Jopati himself had a knife in each hand and fought to protect his two younger brothers, Telso and Kem, each of whom had a small sword. They all expected to die.

The colonel bashar who had killed the Count faced the boys, raised his sword, and laughed. "You show fine mettle, lads. Are you young enough to be trained into something better and strong enough to survive? Or will you foolishly throw your lives away on fruitless revenge?"

Jopati had been so terrified he didn't know how to answer. When he hesitated, the colonel bashar swept his sword sideways, and Jopati held his ground, knowing he was about to die. But the officer controlled his stroke and merely smashed the two knives out of Jopati's hands, leaving him with sore wrists, numb fingers, and nothing else to fight for.

Only later did Jopati learn that the military force consisted of Sardaukar wearing Atreides uniforms so that Duke Paulus would receive the credit, or the blame, for wiping out House Kolona.

The colonel bashar, a steel-hard man named Horthan, took Jopati, Telso, and Kem to the Imperial prison planet, where they were sentenced to be erased, the last members of a rebellious house of the Landsraad. He dumped them inside the oppressive prison complex, but gave them one last chance to survive before torture and execution. Tragically, his youngest brother Kem, only eight years old, died within the first month. Jopati had not seen Kem for days until his bloody and battered body was tossed in front of their cell one night, a tender, barely-alive toy that—to Jopati's rage and disgust—had been passed around among the prisoners.

Jopati and his scrappy twelve-year-old brother Telso did manage to fight off the advances of the prisoners. He was physically strong, athletic in his movements, and quite good with his extended fingers, gouging out the eyes of anyone who tried to come for him or his only remaining brother.

After the two young men passed that first test, Colonel Bashar Horthan took them out of the labyrinthine prison complex. The boys thought they were being rescued when, in fact, their lives would become far worse.

Salusa Secundus, a blistered and windy world that had been devastated in an atomic holocaust by a renegade House millennia earlier, was considered one of the worst planets in the Imperium, a place of fitting punishment for those foolish enough to commit crimes against the Emperor. The prison itself was only part of Salusa's purpose, though. The deadly environment was a testing and training ground to produce the fiercest, most ruthless fighters in the known universe: the Imperial Sardaukar.

Initiation into this elite brotherhood was not so much training as a delayed, agonizing execution, considering how few recruits lived. Early in the horrendous ordeal, the colonel bashar addressed the determined or frightened candidates on a training field in a bleak wasteland. "Long ago, during the reign of Prince Raphael Corrino, the noble House Sardaukar was convicted of plotting against the throne. They were sentenced to Salusa Secundus, where they were expected to die." He swept his gaze across the shivering trainees. "But the ones who lived became the toughest fighters ever.

"Crown Prince Raphael offered them a chance to redeem themselves, when he recruited the surviving lost souls for a desperate military operation, and they saved his rule. Since that time, the greatest fighters serving the Emperor have called themselves *Sardaukar*—not just descendants of that noble House Sardaukar but any prisoners who proved themselves worthy, the survivors of Salusa Secundus." Horthan's stare was like a weapon. "Are you worthy of being Sardaukar?" He looked at all the candidates who stood before him under the harsh sun. "Are you survivors?"

Jopati and the others cheered and made their vows, but later most of them were killed during training, though not the Kolona boys. Horthan took the pair, the last of their Great House, and taught them to fight and survive. He gave them the tools they needed while doing his best to kill them.

In one of their tests, Jopati and Telso were turned loose naked out in a glassy hot canyon; they had to find shelter from fiery windstorms and fight off packs of bloodthirsty predators with nothing but rocks. Surviving that, he and his brother were rewarded with knives, then turned loose to fight the beasts again, more of them this time. Telso survived such ordeals for two years, growing strong and hard, but he died from the bite of a poisonous reptile during group maneuvers—not yet a man by his years, but he died like a man.

Jopati was the only remaining member of House Kolona, unrecognizable from the fresh-faced young man who had hidden in the hills with the Count. All because of the hated Duke Atreides.

Soon even the Kolona family name became buried under scars, blisters, and armor when Colonel Bashar Horthan promoted him to the rank of lieutenant among the Sardaukar, an accomplishment that had more meaning than Jopati's entire family tree.

The Sardaukar had become his family. . . .

THE TALL DATE palms burned in front of the Arrakeen Residency like macabre, smoky candles. On this parched and desolate planet, trees should not have existed at all, but Duke Leto must have had some purpose in keeping the trees where all the people could see them. Flaunting his wealth and water perhaps? Or offering a symbol of hope?

Whatever his thinking, the Duke's plans and dreams would die with him this night. With the house shields sabotaged from within, the Residency was vulnerable to outside attack. The colonel bashar led his forces against a line of hardened Atreides soldiers. The kindjal was Jopati's preferred weapon, a long knife slightly curved, carefully weighted. It was a personal blade, requiring more finesse than a long sword that allowed an attacker to strike from arm's length.

In his false Harkonnen uniform, Jopati faced an Atreides captain, a deeply tanned man with three ornate metal pins on his chest, apparently awards for service or commendations for valor. The captain's uniform cap was askew from when he and his men had rushed out of the troop barracks to form this frantic defense.

Seeing how easily the renowned Atreides fighters had been surprised, the colonel bashar realized a weakness he had not previously considered. Atreides honor was legendary, and Duke Leto's adherence to that core principle had made him a hero among the Landsraad. Leto was revered, celebrated, and even *liked* among the other noble houses, enough to intimidate and annoy Emperor Shaddam IV. But that unwavering devotion to honor also created a blind spot for the Atreides. Despite all their suspicions and precautions, they had not given enough credence to the possibility that one of their own could betray them so completely.

They had a traitor in their midst, someone very close to the Duke.

With his shield belt surrounding him in a comforting hum, Jopati threw himself upon the Atreides captain, his kindjal raised while his opponent defended himself with a longer sword. Their body shields sparked as they crashed into each other. The shimmering Holtzman barrier slowed or deflected any rapid thrust, forcing their desperate battle to become more of a slow dance of blades carefully deflected, points dodging, slashing, stabbing.

"Harkonnen scum!" the captain snarled.

Jopati responded with a hard smile. "You don't even know who you're fighting." He found it insulting to be considered a member of that vile house, but that was part of the plan. Even though Jopati knew he would kill this man, he could not reveal the deception. The Sardaukar had their own code of honor.

The Atreides captain managed to slice his arm with the sword tip, surprising Jopati. He had looked forward to fighting some of the legendary protectors of House Atreides, the troubadour warrior Gurney Halleck, the Swordmaster Duncan Idaho, even the old Mentat, the Master of Assassins Thufir Hawat, but this guard captain was his opponent now. Warm blood trickled down the gray sleeve of his Harkonnen uniform, and he was angry with himself. A Sardaukar should never have been wounded by a mere unnamed captain.

Seeing the splash of blood, tasting just a hint of victory, the Atreides man surged forward. "For the Duke!"

Jopati brought up his kindjal to deflect the blade of his enthusiastic opponent. The body shield blocked what would have been a death blow, and Jopati countered with a much more calculated strike, gliding the kindjal tip through the other man's shield, thrusting into his body slowly, steadily, pushing the tip between the captain's ribs, cutting deeper, all the way into the left side of his chest.

"For the Duke," Jopati whispered as the man died, falling at his feet.

Around him the other disguised Sardaukar dispatched their opponents, leaving dead Atreides soldiers strewn across the Residency grounds. The first ranks of attackers had already broken inside and were swarming through the corridors. By now, Jopati assumed that Duke Leto had been subdued and captured, his concubine and son possibly killed. The Baron would be unable to control his twisted desire for vengeance, but Jopati had his own orders from the Emperor himself, and had to intervene.

He respected the loyalty of the Atreides troops. Few other noble families could command such devotion—Baron Harkonnen certainly didn't! Jopati saw the reason for it himself, and even understood it. He knew from first-hand experience that Duke Leto was no ordinary political leader.

It was not easy to turn against this nobleman.

～⌘～

JOPATI THOUGHT BACK years ago, to a time when he'd held a lower rank. . . .

On Salusa Secundus, in a violent and strictly regimented existence, Jopati Kolona had received a new uniform to go with his fresh commission as a lieutenant. Then, after further years of grooming, he received an assignment more challenging than the most dangerous survival exercises he had faced.

He was sent to Kaitain to become one of the Emperor's elite guard in the Imperial Palace itself.

Though raised as a noble son on Borhees, the new lieutenant now found that he was a stranger to civilization. With their machinations and schemes, the nobles were just as predatory as the poisonous Salusan reptiles, but in a different way. Jopati wore a formal uniform, ate well, and slept in comfortable quarters, but never let his sharp edge of wariness and violence grow dull. His life, loyalty, strength, and skills were sworn in service of the Padishah Emperor, a man who had previously been only a symbol, a name that Colonel Bashar Horthan invoked while shaping the recruits.

Emperor Shaddam IV had ascended to the throne after the death of his father, Elrood IX. Now in his later middle years, Shaddam had reddish hair held in place with delicately scented pomade, an aquiline nose, sharp intense eyes, and thin lips that never smiled. The Emperor loved to surround himself with uniformed Sardaukar and reveled in well-choreographed military parades in the great plaza. Shaddam enjoyed standing at one of his tower windows to watch the precision spectacle from a safe distance without risking interaction with his own subjects.

Jopati had no friends among the Sardaukar, since he had learned not to allow any personal weaknesses. He served as ordered, and because his days in the palace did not involve a constant struggle to survive, he had time—too much time—to remember his murdered family, the destruction of his noble House through the schemes of Duke Paulus Atreides . . . how the guerilla fighters had hidden themselves in the hills, only to be overrun by Sardaukar wearing false Atreides uniforms. He did not understand how Duke Paulus could have been aligned with old Emperor Elrood's wishes.

Though Jopati did not resent what he had become—a far superior human being and an incomparable fighter—his anger toward the Atreides had festered inside him, so much that he did not grieve when he learned that Duke Paulus had been killed in a bullfight, gored to death by a maddened Salusan bull. Yet he felt cheated that he'd not had the opportunity to do it himself. . . .

Years later, hardened into Imperial service and having successfully performed several risky missions to increase Shaddam's power, Jopati had been on duty in the cavernous palace throne room, standing at attention, when he was shocked and disoriented by a supplicant who presented himself before the Golden Lion throne.

Duke Leto Atreides himself.

He was a dark-haired man with gray eyes and hawk features, not dissimilar to Shaddam's appearance. He exuded confidence, having comfortably settled into his role after the death of Duke Paulus. Wearing a civilian suit with the Atreides crest on the jacket, he strode into the throne room in an erect soldierly posture, crossing the expanse of polished stone tiles accompanied by a young man, his bodyguard, introduced as Duncan Idaho. Jopati's fellow Sardaukar guards immediately gauged the potential threat posed by the bodyguard, but Jopati riveted his attention on Leto.

This was the heir to the House that had overthrown his family, that had killed the Count and Countess Kolona and all of Jopati's brothers. This was Duke Leto Atreides, who ruled the planet Borhees as an auxiliary holding, taking the profits for his own coffers on Caladan. Jopati did not doubt that Duke Leto was just as treacherous as his father had been.

Leto paid no attention whatsoever to the Sardaukar guards as he walked up to the throne carved out of a block of Hagal crystal. His bow before Shaddam was polite and respectful but not obsequious. "Cousin, it is good to see you again," Leto said. "It has been awhile since I had personal business on Kaitain."

Jopati narrowed his eyes and felt emotions roil up, hard memories of death and vengeance. He was a loyal Sardaukar, but he was also the last surviving son of the fallen House Kolona.

Shaddam lifted his hands in an impatient gesture, even though Leto was already rising from his bow. "I'm always happy to see you, cousin." Jopati recognized no warmth or welcome in the Emperor's voice. "It is a good sign that you don't come here often, because that means your rule is smooth and without problems. I wish I could say the same of more Landsraad nobles."

Leto smiled. "Perhaps it is because I'm content with my Caladan fief and not desperate to increase the power and influence of House Atreides."

"I wish I could say the same of more Landsraad nobles," Shaddam repeated, then coolly raised his eyebrows. "House Atreides has more holdings than just Caladan, though. You administer the planet Borhees as well. I receive my tithes from you for both worlds, at least according to my treasurer."

Coiled with rage, Jopati did not dare make a move now, could not draw his weapon and attack Leto Atreides before the court, though as a member of the Imperial Sardaukar he had the ability to move throughout the palace. He had allies who would follow his commands without question. He could find a way to abduct Leto, interrogate him, and kill him. Would that be sufficient to balance the scales for House Kolona? Duke Paulus was already dead, but the sudden death of Leto might settle the debt.

The Duke's expression grew more serious. At his side, Duncan Idaho stood stoic and alert, only about eighteen years old but with a great maturity about him. The bodyguard seemed completely content, utterly loyal. Although Idaho was not to be underestimated, Jopati felt certain he could defeat him. Regardless of whether they were evenly matched, Jopati had the added leverage of vengeance and surprise. The young bodyguard didn't know the dark stain on Atreides history.

"Yes, Borhees is a secondary holding of House Atreides," Leto said. "Previously, the planet was administered quite capably by House Kolona, but my father assumed control of the planetary operations twelve years ago." His voice hardened. "In a manner that has always puzzled me, and now I am very disturbed by it."

Jopati tensed but made no move, showed no reaction. The Emperor raised his eyebrows, showing only mild interest.

"I've already presented a petition to the Landsraad," Leto continued. "It is highly unorthodox but perfectly legal, so I see no reason why it will not be approved. I came here as a courtesy to inform you, Sire."

Shaddam frowned, obviously more tense. "What is it you find so important?"

"Due to information recently uncovered, I have come to believe that our administration of Borhees is not legitimate. It always seemed peculiar that my father would have made such an atypical move on such an unusual target. House Atreides did not previously seek expansion beyond Caladan. Then why Borhees? My father only rarely spoke of the matter, and if I ever asked him about it, he seemed genuinely distressed. Once, he told me it was a stain that could not be washed away."

Jopati felt cold inside. His arms were straight at his sides, his hands clenched quietly and unnoticed into fists. The thought of Leto Atreides even speaking his family name seemed like a sacrilege, but the nobleman's words gave Jopati pause. He watched the Emperor's reaction, how he sat on his throne, puzzled and intrigued.

"What nonsense is this? Borhees was granted to House Atreides by right of conquest when your father responded to a ruling. Evidence showed that House Kolona was prepared to go renegade after being accused of embezzling from the Imperial treasury." Shaddam looked down at his fingers as if considering a manicure after the discussion was over. "But that was many years ago. Is Borhees not a profitable holding? Are the people troublesome and causing unrest?"

"No, Sire, neither of those. I have let the people be autonomous. My true home is Caladan."

Shaddam pursed his lips, seeming to grow impatient. Jopati listened in stony silence, wanting to scream out thousands of questions.

Leto said, "In studying my father's records, I came upon some troubling documents. I suspect that the entire operation was not, in fact, instigated by Duke Paulus, and that he merely provided political cover for Emperor Elrood." He paused to let the revelation sink in. "Many of the Kolona holdings were absorbed into the Imperial treasury, though Elrood's name was kept entirely out of it. House Atreides received a substantial payoff for facilitating Elrood's plans and for my father's silence." His hard gaze was locked upon

Shaddam, who sat motionless upon the throne. Leto lowered his voice, speaking in the tone of a friend to his cousin, "I know you had no great love for your father, Sire, and although you had no knowledge of this illegal scheme to crush a member of the Landsraad, it cannot be a complete surprise."

Jopati felt a knot in his stomach. What was this Atreides Duke doing?

"I came here to Kaitain to rectify the situation," Leto said.

Duncan Idaho glanced at his Duke, and the look on his face was one of complete satisfaction, almost bliss.

Shaddam's expression darkened. "Rectify? How?"

Aloof, Leto ran his left hand through his long dark hair. "I have already petitioned the Landsraad Council, releasing details of this unconscionable plot. Any noble House could have been the victim of such a world-grabbing scheme, and they are relieved that your father's ire didn't fall upon them." He straightened. "Although all known members of House Kolona are dead, the Count and Countess and their sons, there are still extended family members who can claim to be legitimate heirs. I offer to return Borhees into their care."

Shaddam half rose from the crystalline throne. "Why would you do that? It paints a shadow across my reign!"

"Not yours, Sire—your father's, and he is long gone. I know that you, dear cousin, would wish to do the moral thing, the *just* thing. The Landsraad members applauded my decision, and I believe they are voting now. We can expect the results soon."

Duncan Idaho's firm lips began to quirk in a small smile. Jopati couldn't believe what he was hearing.

Into Shaddam's stunned silence, Leto continued, "My father hammered into me the idea that honor is the most important thing in any man's heart and mind. I don't know why he was forced to accept the blame and the credit for what he did to House Kolona, but I intend to provide a righteous example if I ever have a son of my own. This is the honorable thing to do. If the Atreides cannot follow the course of honor, then my House is like a Guild ship without a Navigator."

The Emperor could do nothing to stop Leto's plan, because it was already in motion, already publicly announced. If he interfered with the Landsraad vote, Shaddam would look corrupt as well as complicit in what Elrood had done. A masterstroke, Jopati thought, and it would greatly increase Leto's standing among the Landsraad. They would love him for what he had done.

Failing to find a counter argument, the Emperor abruptly dismissed Leto, who bowed again and withdrew with his faithful companion.

Unable to believe or process the startling information he had just heard, Jopati Kolona watched the two Atreides men depart. He felt off-balance, and wondered about the true motivations of Emperor Elrood IX. Previously he had blamed Paulus Atreides for the entire affair, but what if the late Atreides Duke was merely camouflage, coerced into cooperating?

And Leto . . . the young Duke might have kept his silence. In stepping forward, he had everything to lose and nothing to gain.

Except honor.

Jopati decided he might have to reconsider. Perhaps he liked this Duke after all.

THAT HAD BEEN years ago.

Now, following orders, the colonel bashar dispatched his troops throughout the Arrakeen Residency. The fighting continued, and many of his men—Sardaukar!—had been killed in hand-to-hand combat. How could that be possible?

The Atreides were indeed fierce and determined opponents, valiant foes. Thufir Hawat ran the household troops with an iron fist, and against any normal attack by mere Harkonnen troops, they would likely have been victorious. But not against Sardaukar.

By now the Baron Harkonnen's own ship had landed nearby, which he used as his base of operations on Arrakis. As soon as Colonel Bashar Kolona locked down the Residency, he would report to the Baron and insist that he follow the Emperor's orders about the manner of Leto's death. Jopati heard conflicting reports about whether Duke Leto had already been captured or killed in the fighting.

In the courtyard of the Residency, soldiers dragged bodies in Atreides uniforms into lines on the brick pavement, while the fighting continued around the perimeter. Jopati had personally killed twelve during the assault.

Fires burned through the night. Military aircraft cruised across the skies through a maze of smoke columns. Booming rumbles echoed from the fringe of the city where heavy artillery, archaic weaponry deployed by the Harkonnens, pummeled hideout cliffs in the Shield Wall. No one expected such retrograde technology in this day and age, and they were not prepared for it. The Atreides troops who had fallen back to the shelter of the cliffs were being pounded. The dull, booming sounds were like the persistent drumbeat of a funeral procession.

Many of the uniformed troops ransacking the Residency and destroying anything that bore the Atreides hawk crest were real Harkonnen soldiers. Jopati didn't care about them. His Sardaukar troops followed their orders exquisitely, and so did he. He felt unsettled, since the events of this evening reminded him so much of the downfall of House Kolona. The turnabout seemed appropriate and poignant, the perfect way to balance the scales of justice . . . if such scales still needed to be balanced. But Duke Leto Atreides had already settled that score without being coerced, because it was the right and moral thing to do.

Jopati was a Sardaukar officer, but he had no name that anyone remembered or noted. It was not possible for him to rise up, reveal himself and claim the Kolona holdings on Borhees. That possibility had long ago been erased, but he did not yearn for it. He was content with knowing that his relatives had their rightful holdings back. He was a Sardaukar now, so nothing else mattered. He followed the orders of the Padishah Emperor, but he had his own code of honor, a personal compass that guided his actions.

At the far side of the Residency, in the open landing field with guard towers and a small hangar, shouts erupted along with the clang of metal. He saw a furious fight, a lone man in an Atreides uniform against three true Harkonnen troops and two disguised Sardaukar—and the man was holding his own! Jopati jogged forward, saw his other Sardaukar watching the combat with detached interest. They stood with weapons that ranged from heavy launchers to small hand knives. They did not doubt this one man would be defeated, but they marveled at his bravery and fighting finesse. His skill was honed even sharper through desperation.

Jopati recognized the lone Atreides fighter: Swordmaster Duncan Idaho, the man who adhered to the Duke's code of ethics. In precisely controlled strokes, he dipped his blade through the body shield of the nearest Harkonnen fighter and gutted him, then withdrew. With a kindjal in his other hand, he stabbed a Sardaukar in the kidney, a mortal wound. The Sardaukar stumbled, unable to believe the death blow he had just received.

Jopati froze, and the other Sardaukar cried out at the death of their companion.

In efficient fashion, Idaho dispatched the two remaining Harkonnen soldiers and drove back the second Sardaukar, then bolted for the Harkonnen ornithopter on the landing field. Its running lights were still on, its engines powered up.

Along with Jopati, the rest of the Sardaukar in the vicinity lurched into action, no longer just watching the duel. Idaho was a blur of speed, leaving his victims behind. He dove into the cockpit, and without even closing the plaz door, he revved the skimmer engine and set the articulated wings into a blurring flutter of motion.

One Sardaukar reached the ornithopter before Jopati, just as the craft lifted off the ground. The man grabbed for the struts and clung by his fingertips for a few seconds as the 'thopter rose, then he dropped back to the ground from the height of a few meters. More Sardaukar rushed across the landing field, but Idaho had control of the aircraft now. He pulled higher, circling away as he increased speed.

Jopati snatched a large-caliber launcher from one of his fellow soldiers. "Give me that." He wouldn't be fighting the Atreides Swordmaster hand-to-hand, as he had hoped, but he could still shoot down the aircraft with a projectile. Even the fastest 'thopter couldn't outrun an explosive shell. He shouldered the weapon, activated the power pack, and looked through the targeting hairs.

Duke Leto should already be a prisoner. His woman and son must have been captured or killed. After this night, nothing would remain of House Atreides, no more than was left of House Kolona once the Sardaukar swept in and eradicated the guerillas in the hills.

Idaho zigzagged in the air, flying evasive maneuvers, but Jopati knew he could take down the craft. He had his orders. Idaho was only the Atreides Swordmaster, but a high-ranking target nevertheless.

It was not Jopati's decision whether this treacherous attack on the Atreides was just or not. Even if Leto had redeemed himself by restoring the Kolona holdings years ago, too many other events had been set in motion, and Jopati could do nothing for the Duke.

He tracked with the launcher, centering the ornithopter in the targeting crosshairs. The shell was ready, the target in his sights.

He had his orders.

He pressed the ignition stud and launched the projectile, which whistled through the atmosphere in the direction of the fleeing 'thopter.

Colonel Bashar Jopati Kolona knew what Emperor Shaddam expected of him in this night's operation, but the details of the execution were somewhat vague. Jopati was the Sardaukar commander.

And he intentionally missed.

The explosive shell screamed along its trajectory and detonated just shy of Duncan Idaho's craft. Jopati's troops stared after him as the ornithopter sped away, darting among flowering explosions in the sky. The aircraft's running lights went dark as Idaho disappeared into the curling smoke.

Jopati handed the launcher back to the uniformed man who stared at him in silent disbelief, but made no comment. Both the Atreides and Sardaukar had codes of honor.

Gesturing toward his men in Harkonnen uniforms, the colonel bashar marched them into the Residency for one last encounter with Duke Leto Atreides.

THE
WATERS
OF KANLY

From the Lost Years
of Gurney Halleck

Blood is thicker than water.
Water is more precious than spice.
Revenge is most precious of all.
　　　　—songs of Gurney Halleck

I

The baliset strings thrummed and the flywheel spun, producing a sad song . . . as it always did.

Gurney Halleck used the multipick, focused on the music that came from his beloved instrument, immersed in the mood, the sorrow, the anger. With the music, he didn't need to think about the crackling dry air, the rock-walled caves of the smugglers' hideout, the grief that had set deeply into his bones, still undiminished even after a full year.

Harkonnen forces had swept into the Atreides stronghold in Arrakeen as soon as the household shields were dropped, thanks to an as-yet unidentified traitor, no doubt someone trusted . . . and deadly. Gurney was convinced that person was the she-witch Jessica, and because of her, Duke Leto was dead. Young Master Paul was dead, too, as was the loyal Duncan Idaho, a master fighter like Gurney.

And so, if reports were to be believed, was Jessica herself.

After the Harkonnens had once again taken over Arrakis, the planet commonly known as Dune, Gurney Halleck was the only surviving Atreides lieutenant, he and 73 other men. The Atreides Mentat, Thufir Hawat, had been captured alive and was now forced to serve the vile Baron Harkonnen. Only Gurney and his men remained free, and they spoke often of seeking revenge.

But it was difficult and long delayed.

He let the emotions flow as he sang a sad refrain. . . .

> "A man of his people, not of himself,
> Duke Leto betrayed, oh how can it be?
> Of all the nobles, why our gallant Duke?
> I shall never forget, shall never forgive . . ."

Gurney looked up as a shadow fell over him, cast by the light of the glowglobes suspended near the rock ceiling. A burly man stood a head taller than Gurney with blocky features that looked as if they had been carved from lava rock by an inexpert sculptor who had imbibed too much spice beer. Orbo was one of the reliable smugglers who had served their leader Staban Tuek for years, a muscular man who excelled in physical endurance and strength, but was never called upon to do much thinking.

Gurney kept playing absently, though his singing faltered into silence as he saw the angry expression on Orbo's face. The large group sat inside the rock-walled assembly hall of the smugglers' hideout, their improvised sietch in the deep desert. The natural caves had been cut deeper with heavy equipment, the living chambers outfitted to look like the cabins and piloting deck of a spice freighter.

Many of Gurney's men were in the assembly room playing gambling games, talking about their long-lost homes on Caladan, describing their prowess with women from bygone days. Few discussed business, because Staban Tuek was the one who determined the time and the place of their raids, and his smugglers followed his orders.

Gurney's fingers stilled on the baliset strings. Orbo's face rippled with uneasiness and anger, as he seemed to be having difficulty articulating what was upsetting him.

"Don't you have a fondness for music, man?" Gurney asked. He realized that the big muscular man had often shown discomfort whenever he played and sang.

"Oh, I like music all right," Orbo said in a voice thick from a lifetime of breathing and speaking dust. "I just don't like your music. I want happy music, joyful music." He scowled. "Your songs have too much anger, too much revenge."

Gurney's eyes narrowed. This man was treading on dangerous ground and could get hurt for doing so, no matter his size. "Perhaps vengeance is the most important I have to sing about . . . after what House Harkonnen did."

Orbo shook his head. "We are smugglers and have no time for politics. You are dangerous."

With the palm of his hand Gurney stopped the flywheel spinning. "When my men and I joined you, I swore to Staban I would delay my revenge and find an appropriate way, but I never promised to forget about it entirely." His voice hitched, but he clamped down on his emotions. "Thinking about revenge keeps me going."

Orbo seized the baliset, snatching it right out of his hands. Gurney grabbed for it, but the big man swung the old instrument and drove it hard against the heat-smoothed stone wall. He smashed the instrument, causing it to make a discordant jangle, like ghosts of the saddest songs ever sung. With an angry grunt, he tossed the string-tangled splinters in a heap at Gurney's feet. "Now you don't have music either, and we can finally have peace."

At another time, Gurney would have murdered him on the spot. He tightened his jaw, making the inkvine scar there ripple and dance like a purplish dying snake. Several of the other Atreides survivors rose to their feet, casting deadly glances toward Orbo as he stalked off. Gurney raised a hand, stopping them. He quelled his own anger, walling it off into a safe internal compartment, as he'd been doing since that terrible night.

Staban Tuek emerged from a small side chamber he used as an office, his expression dark. First looking at the departing Orbo and then at the wrecked instrument on the floor, he asked, "What have you done now, Gurney Halleck?"

Gurney struggled to control himself. *Everything in its time, and there is a time for everything.* "As I sit here with my prized possession ruined, your first thought is to ask me what *I've* done?"

"Yes, I do." He glanced at the tunnel where Orbo had vanished. "That man doesn't have the imagination to be cruel. You must have done something to irritate him. *Seriously* irritate him."

Gurney twitched his fingers as if he could still play an imaginary baliset. "Apparently some of your men don't like sad songs."

The smuggler leader snorted. "None of us do. And we're growing pretty tired of you." His expression softened and he gave a hint of a smile to mitigate his words. "You obsess on the defeat of your House Atreides rather than victories to come. You and your men are smugglers now and should be thinking of raiding spice, developing black markets, and stealing equipment from the Harkonnens to sell back to them at exorbitant prices." Staban shook his head. "The past is the past. And remember what I told you when you first came to me after the fall of Arrakeen, when you were burned and dirty, weak and starving."

"The same night your own father was murdered by the Harkonnen monsters," Gurney said.

Staban twitched, but narrowed his gaze and focused his words. "I gave you a home but I warned you not to seek revenge too soon, bringing down the anger of our new planetary masters, House Harkonnen. As my father said, 'A stone is heavy and the sand is weighty; but a fool's wrath is heavier than both.'"

"I remember the quote," Gurney muttered, "but I prefer another from Esmar Tuek." He smiled, softening the features on his lumpy face. "'There's more than one way to destroy a foe.'" He kicked the jangling wires and debris of his baliset as if it meant nothing to him. Compared to his plans, the lost instrument was indeed a trivial thing. Revenge against the Harkonnens, against the loathsome acting governor Beast Rabban was paramount. "I've been pondering something in the Orange Catholic Bible, 'A thinking man has infinite options, but a reactive man is doomed to only one path.'"

"You always have a quote. One for every occasion, it seems. Now what the hell does that one mean?"

"It means I have an idea about how to hurt Rabban, one that should also prove profitable for us."

Tuek was intrigued. "I much prefer this line of thinking. Tell me."

Gurney brushed himself off and walked with the smuggler leader back to his office, speaking in a low voice. "Regular shipments of supplies and equipment come from offworld to Rabban's garrison city of Carthag. The Beast should not be entitled to all of them." He paused, letting the idea sink in. He could see the thoughts churning on Staban's face.

"First," Gurney continued, "we have to arrange a meeting with the Emperor's unofficial ambassador to the smugglers."

II

As far as Gurney was concerned, this was not a man to be trusted.

Count Hasimir Fenring was a weasel-faced, dithering imperialist who held a great deal of power. Apparently, Fenring had been a childhood friend of the Padishah Emperor Shaddam IV. They had shared many schemes and violent adventures, and according to rumor had even assassinated Shaddam's father, placing the Crown Prince on the throne. On the surface, Fenring had the ability to seem innocuous and foppish, with a meandering conversational style, yet he had a gaze like a pair of surgical needles. This was a deadly killer and the Emperor's proxy on Arrakis. Gurney knew well, he was not a man to be underestimated, and might even have been involved in the plot to destroy House Atreides.

Fenring had come to Carthag on official business, to meet with Glossu Rabban and ensure that after a full year the Harkonnen spice-harvesting operations were producing the expected amounts of the valuable melange, found only in the deep deserts of this planet. Count Fenring had countless unofficial dealings on the Emperor's behalf, of which neither the Harkonnens nor the Landsraad nobles knew anything. Because of his illicit interactions with smuggler bands such as Staban Tuek's, he held the whispered, unofficial title of "Ambassador to the Smugglers."

Carthag, a brassy and blustery new city thrown together with prefabricated buildings and no finesse, was a place of dark alleys and sharp corners where Harkonnen troops held as much power over the populace as they could grab, a city where happiness was a rare and expensive commodity.

Through his connections among the merchants and military

quartermasters in Carthag, Staban had slipped Count Fenring a
message, and the count had arranged this meeting in an airlocked
bar down a side alley, where the price of water was more expensive
than any exotic or extravagant alcoholic drink. The proprietor had
paid substantial bribes to Harkonnen guards and officials to ensure
that this low-profile drinking establishment remained unharassed,
the patrons allowed a small measure of privacy.

Gurney and Staban wore dusty desert robes, and Gurney kept a
stillsuit mask across his face and a cowl around his head, while Staban was more brash, confident that no one would recognize him . . .
or at least no one would care. Eerie warbling semuta music played
in the background. Incense wafted pinkish clouds of aroma into the
stuffy air. All manner of dusty, dirty patrons filled the bar, many
of whom were engaged in whispered conversations, as if they were
plotting something illegal.

A man entered through the door seal, and Gurney recognized
Fenring, the Imperial representative, a man with secrets and goals
of his own. He wore traditional local garb without Harkonnen
military markings: drab and dusty folds of cloth, a breathing mask
across his face, but he didn't seem to belong here. At first Gurney
thought that Fenring—with his fine upbringing and noble ways—
was just uncomfortable in a seedy place like this, but realized as
Fenring's close-set eyes flashed that this wasn't the case at all. No,
the part of Fenring that didn't belong was an act. At any moment he
could glide into the shadows with a dagger or other weapon and do
exactly what needed to be done, without flinching or the slightest
remorse.

Staban signaled him with a subtle hand gesture, and Fenring
glided over with a jouncey step. He sat on a hard chair, removed his
head covering. Gurney and Staban already had their drinks, diluted
spice beers.

Fenring lifted a finger as the surly, wrung-out waitress came up
to him. "Ah, I would like water please. Purified water of course, but
with a splash of citrus flavoring. Let's make it special tonight for this
meeting, hmmm?"

"Water," she said. "I'll see if I can find something to add taste."

Though Staban had requested the meeting, Fenring took charge, leaning over the table, glancing at Gurney without recognition but focusing his piercing gaze on the smuggler leader. "I have come to oversee Governor Rabban's activities here. I fear he will not do well, hmmm."

"We hope that is the case," Gurney muttered.

Fenring suddenly paid attention to him. They had met previously, a brief occasion when Gurney was with Duke Leto, but the Count showed no indication of knowing this. Still, something seemed to be nagging at him, tickling his memory. "Interesting . . . hmmm."

Staban sucked in a breath and interrupted. "We don't care who the planetary governor is, so long as we are able to perform our own work, unmolested."

"And that is why I do business with you, my dear Staban, ahhh," Fenring said. "For all the good intentions—or bad—of the new Harkonnen overlords, the Padishah Emperor does not like a bottleneck in the flow of spice, nor does he care for a single disreputable source of melange. Imperial governors are so notoriously . . . ummm . . . unreliable. After all, look what happened to poor Duke Atreides, hmmm?"

Gurney felt a flush of angry heat through his skin, took a deep breath for courage. He reached up and removed the nostril plugs, the covering over his mouth, slid down the cowl to expose the prominent inkvine scar on his cheek, the scar that Rabban himself had inflicted upon him after the horrible rape and beating he had committed against Gurney's sister, right before his very eyes . . . "Yes, look what happened to the Atreides. Look what happened to my Duke." He waited a beat as Fenring studied him, worked through his thoughts and memories, tried to recognize who Gurney was.

"You are one of the Duke's men. A well-known one, hmmm." He pursed his lips, "Ah yes, Halleck, isn't it?"

"Gurney Halleck."

"Most unfortunate what happened to your Duke, yes, most unfortunate, indeed. And I'm not surprised some of the Duke's men survived, though I am surprised that you would fall in among the smugglers."

"I had few choices," Gurney answered in a growl. He sipped his diluted spice beer, and the waitress shuffled over with Fenring's water. It looked murky from some oily additive. Fenring sipped, grimaced, but thanked the waitress anyway.

"The Atreides fell, and it was not entirely due to the Harkonnens. There was treachery." Gurney leaned over the table. "Was it treachery from the Emperor?"

Fenring looked astonished by the suggestion. Staban reacted with alarm, said, "He didn't mean that, sir—"

The Count glared at Gurney. "I assure you, hmmm, that the Emperor takes no part in the petty squabbles of Landsraad nobles."

Gurney rested his elbows on the table. "Then we must have been imagining things when we fought enemies in Harkonnen livery who were quite clearly trained as Sardaukar."

Fenring paused for a moment too long before saying, "Then the Baron must have hired some mercenaries with excellent training."

Gurney didn't believe him for a moment, but let the matter drop. Fenring knew something, though he probably was not involved in the planning. As a minimum, he and the Emperor looked the other way and let the Harkonnens commit their treachery. He took a deep calming breath. That assessment wasn't his focus right now. "Politics and politics," he said, "and damn it all to the Seven Hells. I know who the traitor was—Jessica, the concubine of my beloved Duke, the woman who shared his bed, the mother of—" His voiced hitched. "The mother of Paul Atreides, dear Paul. All of them gone now." He drew a deep breath, felt his face flush. "There must be an accounting against the Harkonnens, sir." His voice was hard and determined, and across the table from him Fenring's eyes bored into his, like a laser cutter. "Even before House Atreides moved to this damned desert planet, we knew there was a plot. We knew the Duke's enemies had gathered against him. Duke Leto Atreides formally declared kanly on the Baron Vladimir Harkonnen. There are rules and expectations to that ancient blood feud." Gurney waited a beat. "And now I insist on my right. Sir, on behalf of my fallen House and my noble Duke, I demand satisfaction."

Fenring's eyes lit up, and a sardonic smile curled at the edges of his mouth. He sat back, took another unconscious sip of the murky water. "Yes, rules, hmmm. Rules."

"I demand that the forms be obeyed."

"But, ahhh, Duke Leto is dead now," Fenring pointed out. "As is his son and heir Paul."

"I know. And when all the lights go out, darkness only wins until another flame lights the shadows. I am the Duke's last remaining lieutenant. I claim the right of kanly. I will finish this battle against House Harkonnen—in my own way."

Fenring let out a long and weary sigh and drained half of his water in one gulp. "Hmmm, vows of revenge are so tedious, so boring to me. Is that why you brought me here?"

Staban Tuek quickly broke in, looking uneasy. "My companion focuses too much on revenge and forgets the more relevant part of this discussion. He has developed a plan of action—a fascinating one, I think you'll agree.

"The Harkonnens supply Rabban's military outpost in Carthag with offworld water, shipped from their homeworld, Giedi Prime. The water costs little, although the transportation is expensive. A supply tanker of water, enough to fulfill the extravagant needs of the Harkonnen troops, arrives each month. To the people on Giedi Prime, it is mere water, practically free. To the people of Arrakis, it is a treasure worth more than spice. For some it is worth more than life itself."

"We intend to hijack the tanker and take the water," Gurney interrupted, catching Fenring's attention again. "We need to enlist your assistance, your connections, Count Fenring. We require access to the Guild Heighliner. When it arrives, we need to know the crew and defenses aboard the Harkonnen tanker when it's still up in orbit. Once we get aboard, we'll handle the rest."

Staban interjected, "Stealing that tanker will be a great embarrassment for Rabban—and thus Gurney gets his revenge and can declare kanly complete. And we smugglers receive a water prize worth a huge amount of solaris here on Arrakis."

Fenring sounded dubious. "And why would I assist you in this? What possible reason would I have?"

Gurney chose to state the matter flat out. "Because we will pay you an enormous bribe."

Staban looked as if he had just swallowed sand, and choked on it.

Fenring did not laugh, nor dismiss the suggestion. "And the Guild itself will require tremendous payments, hmmmm." He tapped his fingers on the tabletop. "I admit there is a measure of amusement in placing Rabban in an awkward position. It is never good to have a planetary governor who grows too complacent. Giving him a black eye could be very beneficial."

Gurney knotted and unknotted his fists on the table. "We will pay the inducement. We will round up additional spice, and you will have the funds you need."

"I haven't even quoted the price yet, hmmm. You may find it overwhelming."

"We will pay it," Gurney said, and Staban glared at him. Fenring's eyes narrowed, flicking back and forth as he performed calculations in his mind. Gurney was reminded of how Thufir Hawat had concentrated with remarkable focus and intensity, when he performed Mentat projections.

Then Fenring quoted an amount so astronomical that Staban gasped and looked at him in disbelief. Gurney had made calculations of his own, knowing the smugglers and the Atreides fighters would find ways to gather extra spice in their raids, perhaps with the cooperation of desert villagers, maybe even the Fremen.

"We will pay it," Gurney said again.

III

It was not difficult to rally the desert villagers and the Fremen against the Harkonnens. Gurney had known it wouldn't be. He knew Beast Rabban.

Less than a week after their secret meeting with Fenring, smuggler scouts and spice hunters on the edge of the desert plateau spotted a black flag of smoke curling up from the elbow of a canyon, the site of one of the hardscrabble graben villages. A squalid town that collected droplets of moisture from the air with huge skimmers and condensers, people who coaxed useful minerals and metals from the rocks and scavenged just enough spice from the open desert to trade in the cities for supplies and medicines they needed, and no luxuries. The smoke had wafted up, dissipating for hours before a spotter reported it.

After checking the weather report and verifying there were no sandstorms or turbulent cyclones on the flight path, Gurney flew the low-altitude ornithopter. Beside him, a concerned-looking Orbo rode, along with Staban and ten other armed smugglers in seats at the back, all clad in desert gear. Even after being stranded here for a year in the smuggler crew, Gurney still found it awkward to prepare for combat without a personal shield, but no one on Arrakis wore a shield. Not only did the sand and dust make the devices malfunction, the pulsing field-effect would invariably attract and madden a giant sandworm.

No amount of personal protection was worth the risk of facing a monster like that.

Gruff Orbo looked through the 'thopter's scratched and pitted plaz window as Gurney flew in toward the smoke.

Once or twice he had considered challenging the bigger man

to a duel, to slay him in front of the other smugglers for the insult of smashing the baliset. The smuggler caves were without music now, and Gurney found them a much sadder, lonelier place. But he knew that if he challenged Orbo, who had many friends among the smugglers, he would damage his own standing in the group. Even if he won the duel, he would have to leave. Gurney didn't want that, couldn't afford it. He needed these hardened smugglers, especially now that he was so close to achieving what he wanted so badly. He had not forgiven Orbo, but gave the matter no further thought now, blocking it away like putting it inside a walled fortress. He did not allow the incident to fester within him the way the thought of Rabban did.

The way the traitor Jessica festered within him.

"I know what *that* place is," Orbo said, pointing down at the surface. The rattling hum of the engine and flutter of the articulated wings nearly drowned out his voice.

Gurney looked to the side, through the window past Orbo. "What is it? What's out there?"

Orbo simply stared out the window.

Just behind Gurney, Staban leaned close. "His village is out there. He came from the desert people and joined us. Sometimes we bring water and supplies to that settlement."

As Gurney flew in, he realized with a sinking sensation what the curling smoke meant. "Looks like someone else found it, too."

Orbo just stared gloomily. He'd already figured this out himself.

The smugglers were greatly uneasy as Gurney brought the 'thopter around the high cliffs and into the elbow canyon. Black starbursts of explosions marked the desert floor and cliff walls. The once-huddled buildings of the small outpost had been smashed and burned. Bodies lay sprawled in the streets, their skin blackened, some of their desert stillsuits still smoldering as slow-burning fires ate through the sandwiched fabric and cooked the dead flesh underneath.

Gurney had barely landed the 'thopter when Orbo cracked open the door and burst out, his boots sinking into the stirred gravel and sand. He didn't even affix his nose plugs or breathing mask. He bounded forward, letting out primal sounds as the other smugglers followed.

Gurney shut down the rotors, racked the articulated wings into their resting position, then joined Staban outside. While Orbo and the smugglers searched the mangled remnants of huts, the low dwellings built into cliff walls, and the supply sheds that had been leveled with explosives, frantically looking for survivors, Gurney knew they would find none. Rabban would not have left any.

Orbo came back, his face distraught. Soot smeared his cheeks and desert cloak. Other smugglers had dragged out the bodies of dead villagers, laying them out on the bleak canyon floor.

"Who did this?" Orbo sobbed. "Why?"

"You know who did it," Gurney said. "Perhaps your people didn't pay Rabban the tithes he demanded, or maybe his men were just bored."

"No survivors?" Staban asked.

"They're all dead. He wanted to burn everything so no one would find this village at all. A single sandstorm can wipe out the rest of the evidence."

"Rabban doesn't care about any evidence he leaves behind," Gurney said. "He's perfectly happy to let you find it. Dozens of other villages in the pan and graben have suffered the same fate in the past year. Rabban needs to make everyone fear him." He clenched his jaw. "Any fool would know this is wasteful, not leadership."

When he glanced up, he caught a flicker of movement in the cliffs, in the shadows of rock, while a figure, a human figure, darted into a cleft. As Gurney watched, a camouflage cloak swirled up and he could no longer see the person.

"Fremen," Staban muttered.

Gurney was intrigued. "An eyewitness, maybe?"

"More likely just drawn to the smoke to investigate—and to scavenge what he can."

Gurney looked down at the bodies lined up outside the village, recalling a rumor he'd heard that Fremen took dead bodies and extracted the water from their flesh. Yes, water was indeed a precious commodity here. If Gurney and the smugglers hadn't flown in, maybe the Fremen would have stolen the bodies so that no one knew what happened to them. He looked around at the cliffs, saw no further movement, could no longer see a hint of where the furtive Fremen had vanished. He suspected others were also watching, camouflaged as well. They would be listening.

Gurney looked at Orbo, then at the smuggler leader, and spoke loudly. "Staban, this is the time for revenge. You have made me wait too long. Now Orbo's village is destroyed, his entire family. Staban, your father is also dead because of the Harkonnens." He raised his voice to a shout, "And all you Fremen, I know you're listening. Spread the word among your sietches. Tell the desert people in the graben villages and those hidden in the deepest wilds that we need a huge amount of spice . . . not for our own profit, but to make the proper bribes. Tell them we have a way to hurt the Beast who did this."

Gurney knew if his words resonated here, the message would spread. The survivors and bereaved from other villages Rabban had preyed upon . . . those people would help him. He wasn't the only one with justification for a vendetta. So much blood had been spilled that the cost in spice was not even worth measuring.

They had three weeks to raise the enormous amount of melange before Count Fenring returned.

They would get more than they needed in two.

IV

Twelve men, all loyal, tried-and-true Atreides veterans for the mission.

Gurney selected them himself and disappointed others back in the smugglers' hideout, because every one of his men who had survived Arrakeen still served the memory of their beloved Duke Leto and his family, and wanted to share in Gurney Halleck's quest to meet the requirements of kanly. They all wanted to shed Harkonnen blood, but he could only take a small number on the mission up to the Guild Heighliner, where they would steal Rabban's water tanker. A dozen men following him . . . and Gurney didn't promise they would survive. He merely told them they might, and might not die. Brave and dedicated men, that was good enough for them.

"For House Atreides!" they called out in a cheer, joined by the other Atreides men who had failed to make the cut.

Staban Tuek then insisted that Gurney also take six of his original smugglers to ensure his own profit as well as Gurney's vengeance. Orbo led this smaller group, but they would follow Gurney's orders, to complete his plan.

The squad traveled surreptitiously to the battle-damaged spaceport at Arrakeen, much smaller than the large industrial platforms in Rabban's city of Carthag. Following the attack a year ago, using modern weapons and old-style artillery, the Harkonnen invaders had damaged much of the Arrakeen spaceport, and although it had been patched and repaired to make it serviceable, no one had bothered to clean up all the battle debris, not thinking it mattered.

That's how the Harkonnens were, and Carthag was their capital here, while Arrakeen was just a sad and painful memory of the all-too-brief Atreides rule. Gurney wanted to depart from the Arrakeen spaceport for a purpose, though. He despised Carthag and the pigsty stink of Harkonnens there. The frontier town of Arrakeen was more familiar to him, and more appropriate for the purpose of kanly.

The forms must be obeyed, he thought.

By his reaction, Count Fenring had obviously been surprised to receive the enormous spice bribe he'd demanded. The amount was so exorbitant he'd never imagined that even the largest smuggling crew could achieve it, but he accepted the shipment with good grace and no questions. In return, he provided the vital information Gurney had requested, Guild access cards, stolen uniforms, codes and schedules . . . basics that the raid required.

Gurney had led his own men into battle many times. They were well versed in Atreides code language, and would follow his orders instantly and efficiently. They understood his tactics instinctively, and never questioned an order in the slightest degree. He spent more of his time discussing the plan with Orbo and Staban's men, all of whom gruffly acknowledged his instructions. They could smell profit and the adrenaline-rush of adventure. The thought of seizing an entire Harkonnen tanker filled with water destined for Rabban's troops filled them with excitement and anticipation.

Back on Caladan, Gurney had often listened to half-drunk men in dockside taverns sharing preposterous stories about great fish they had nearly caught out on the sea, but had gotten away. The water tanker would be like that in Gurney's secret plan, unrevealed to them, or to anyone else. His plan within a plan.

This big fish would get away . . . or it would seem to do so.

The men were silent, huddled with excitement and wrapped in desert clothes like refugees as they rode together in the rumbling liner that lifted off from the Arrakeen spaceport. The Guild pilot asked no questions of his passengers, merely acknowledged that their documents were correct and their passage was paid for, along with the additional bribe Gurney had paid to him, to ensure the man's best work. Few workers were able to buy their way off the desert planet, particularly now that Rabban had clamped down on veteran spice crews in order to increase production, but Gurney had found a way to circumvent the system.

The Duke's man knew that all necessary details were in order; Staban Tuek had enough connections to make it so. The only questionable part about their disguises, he realized, was that these men were intent and grim—and any workers truly escaping from Arrakis would be celebrating. But none of his team could find it within their hearts to fake that part, even though it had been suggested.

The lighter was an old-model ship with few amenities. Gurney gripped the armrests of his worn seat, holding himself against violent tremors as the craft heaved itself out of the planet's gravity well like an old man rising roughly to his feet. Through thick plaz portholes he could see the cracked scab of the desert dwindling below, smeared and softened by a haze of high, orangish dust. He turned his gaze upward to where the sky darkened and the atmosphere thinned toward space and the huge Guild Heighliner waited for them.

His pulse raced. Plans and memories collided in his mind, and his fingers twitched involuntarily, as if playing the strings of an imaginary baliset.

His men muttered to one another, pretending to make idle conversation but listening to few of the words. An island in their midst, Gurney focused his thoughts forward, reviewing each step they would take once they reached the huge ship.

The Heighliner's enormous hold carried countless separated vessels on docking cradles. A Guild navigator would fold space and transport the immense ship from star system to star system, stopping along the way so that smaller ships could disembark and fly to their destinations.

But first, Gurney had something to do. . . .

The lighter rising from Arrakeen reached orbit less than an hour after the huge Heighliner arrived. Gurney had complete confidence in Fenring's information, but he also had every reason not to trust the man. *Visionaries and fools feed themselves on optimism, not bread.* Even so, Gurney thought he could rely on Fenring to get them inside the big vessel. After that, he would count on nothing but the skill, dedication and courage of his best men.

The lighter came aboard the huge ship, maneuvered into the central hold as the great bay doors opened and the administration work took place, with Guild officials accounting for all arriving craft, assigning docking cradles, finishing documentation so that the outbound vessels could depart for Arrakis.

According to Fenring, the bribe to the Guild was enough for them to bureaucratically stall the release of Rabban's water tanker.

"We won't have much time," Gurney said to his men, repeating what he'd told them earlier.

Orbo held his hands in front of his face, palms facing and fingers curled, as if he were thinking of strangling a succession of enemies. He had been murderously gloomy ever since seeing the massacre of his village by Rabban's troops.

The lighter docked, its slender form clicking into the clamp, and the egress tube deployed from the Heighliner wall, connecting to the main hatch of the lighter. Gurney motioned to his men that it was time. When the hatch opened he led his team through the connecting tube, shucking their dusty and tattered desert cloaks along the way because they would not need them again. Beneath their traditional clothes, they wore the Guild uniforms Fenring had obtained. Gurney had used makeup over the inkvine scar on his face, but his lumpy features and characteristic rolling gait could never be concealed from anyone familiar with him.

Gurney intended to kill any Harkonnen who showed the slightest inkling of recognizing him. And if they didn't show any such sign, he would still kill them, though perhaps not so quickly. Fortunately for him, many Guildsmen also had imperfect features. He felt comfortable on their huge ship; he was fitting in well.

Once away from the lighter, Gurney consulted the detailed schematic of the vessel that Fenring and the Guild had provided. His men had to work their way through the inner hull decks of the Heighliner to find the Harkonnen water tanker, a trivial ship among the thousands of vessels carried by this enormous transport.

Inside the sandwiched hull decks they rode tube transports, sitting alongside silent Guildsmen who showed no interest in their presence. Gurney's squad traveled along the hull, rising up the curve, counting decks until they reached the appropriate sector that contained the docking clamp holding the water tanker.

Gurney and the uniformed men carried packs, tool kits, diag-

nostics, and false documents showing that they had been sent to inspect the manifest of the Harkonnen transport. All perfectly routine. Gurney knew none of the Harkonnen crew would be suspicious because they were arrogant. His men also carried packs with hidden weapons, knives and maula pistols as well as personal shields—which were never used down in the desert, but Gurney insisted on them here. This would be his kind of fight, and on his terms, his own retaliatory sneak attack.

Gurney also had a special surprise inside his pack, something required by the kanly he intended to administer.

His men were subdued and intense, their eyes shining and deep blue from frequent consumption of the spice melange. This distinctive tint might have been problematic, except Guildsmen also imbibed spice heavily. In all likelihood no one would question the coloration . . . at least not before his team had their chance.

Gurney felt a rush of relief as they came upon the access ramp assigned to the Harkonnen water tanker. Gurney used his access cards, having no choice except to hope Fenring and his Guild allies had deflected the previously assigned Guild inspection teams, leaving the way open for him and his crew. As a matter of practice, the Spacing Guild did not involve themselves in petty family feuds, especially not something so small as a single water tanker . . . and certainly not an outburst from the last remnants of a fallen noble house of the Landsraad. House Atreides was irrelevant to them, but it was not irrelevant to Gurney or to any of his men.

Staban's six smugglers were efficient enough, and businesslike, but the Atreides men were on a higher level, more intense. Orbo almost had that, impressing Gurney a bit, but not causing him to let down his guard. He recalled something the assassinated Duke Leto had said to him once, that "an enemy can be anywhere, declared or undeclared."

At the end of the ramp, the hatch opened to the tanker, and they boarded through the lower deck. Inside, a surly-looking engineer stood with arms crossed over his wide chest, a frown on his face. The griffin symbol and the colors of House Harkonnen drove a knot into Gurney's stomach, but he maintained a neutral expression.

"About damn time," the engineer said. "We need to depart within the hour. Do your inspections and sign off on the paperwork."

"We'll be faster if you leave us to our own work," Gurney said.

"All right, go about it, then," said the Harkonnen engineer. "I have enough of my own damn' work trying to take this load down to Carthag. The captain says there's been a security alert on the Heighliner, and we've all had to do nonsense drills. I don't have time to show you around anyway."

Gurney felt a chill, and his men flicked glances at one another. One twitched toward his pack and the weapons hidden there, but Gurney made a subtle gesture to calm him.

"We'll be efficient," he said. "I just need to see your cargo hold, and these men will verify your atmospheric engines."

Showing impatience, the engineer pointed them in various directions for the inspections.

"Security alert, Gurney?" muttered one of his men, as soon as the engineer was out of earshot. "Do you think we've been betrayed?"

"There's always a chance of that, but I've heard that security alerts are commonplace on Heighliners. This is a fresh crew. Did you see the water fat on his face? He's never been to Arrakis before."

The other man grumbled, "No appreciation for water, that's for sure."

Gurney nodded. "All to our advantage. Now go."

The men split up, going about their "Guild inspection" duties. Their uniforms made them invisible to the Harkonnen crew. Gurney hoped they didn't have to begin killing before it was time, or that could alert others. Fenring had instructed Gurney not to make any move until the water tanker dropped out of the Heighliner's hold and was free of Guild jurisdiction—he had made the importance of that eminently clear.

Acting his part as "Chief Cargo Inspector," Gurney made his way to the lower bulkhead that sealed the bulbous compartment holding a large bubble of water—water from Giedi Prime, a place where such a substance was as unremarkable as air, a shipment that cost the Baron Harkonnen almost nothing, yet was worth an incredible treasure here on Arrakis.

Plaz observation ports providing them with views into the cargo hold showed only murky liquid, but Gurney knew its potential, its worth. This water represented *revenge* to him. Kanly. It represented hope, and death. A smile twitched across his face.

He found an access port for drawing samples and testing the water, but from the look of things Gurney doubted the tanker captain had ever bothered to do this himself. These Harkonnens did not yet have an appreciation for the value of water on the driest, most desolate planet in the universe.

He unshouldered his pack and got to work, doing his secret thing, the thing that even his most trusted followers did not know about.

When it was done, Gurney stared at the precious cargo behind the plaz observation window, but he thirsted for something else.

V

It was easy enough to fool the tanker's systems. Playing their role as Guild functionaries, Gurney and his men verified the craft's engines, acknowledged the cargo of water, signed off on the tanker's departure from the Heighliner. An hour later, after most of the other Arrakis-bound ships had already dropped from their docking cradles and descended to the desert planet, the water tanker was at last cleared. The Guild inspectors departed through the access tube into the main ship again—at least that was what the records showed—and the tanker captain received authorization to depart.

But after Gurney and his team supposedly left the access tube, two of his men remained behind, hidden on the engineering deck, where they could divert the sensors on the sealed door. When clear, they let the fighters back in, and they rushed to take hiding places among the engine blocks and cooling racks. Gurney knew it was an inelegant hiding place, but they needed only ten minutes before the tanker dropped out of the Heighliner and began its spiral toward the desert planet on course to Carthag.

Huddled in the dark and noisy lower decks, they heard the thump and felt the jarring vibration through the hull as the tanker drifted free. Slow suspensor engines guided it carefully among the other stowed vessels within the Guild ship's hold, then the tanker dropped out into open space over the desert planet. The more powerful engines ignited, driving it down toward Arrakis.

Gurney's heart raced as if he had taken a heavy dose of stimulants. Revenge was his stimulant. All of his men felt the same. Orbo's hooded brow shaded his gleaming eyes, and he continued to strangle imaginary foes.

Concealing himself among the conduits and cooling tubes, Gurney held his breath, counting silently as the tanker dropped away from the Heighliner. When he knew it was safe, Gurney gestured to his team. They attached their shield belts, clipping them into place but not activating them yet. After he closed his eyes and breathed a prayer, he raised a hand, and his men surged out of their places of concealment.

They moved out, knowing their one goal was to reach the piloting deck and seize control of the tanker. According to Fenring, only seven Harkonnen crew would be on the bridge, four more down in engineering, and two more in other duties around the tanker. Gurney had enough fighters to overrun them, and he had the element of surprise.

The impatient engineer was the first man they encountered. "You're not supposed to be—"

One of the smugglers fired a maula pistol, and the projectile ripped through the engineer's chest. The boom of the spring-wound weapon was loud, but mostly drowned out by engine noise. Another engineer shouted, calling for help. Gurney ran straight at him, holding his knife in one hand. He preferred to use the more personal touch of death, because this was a very personal matter. He bounded ahead as the astonished second engineer turned to flee, grabbed the man by the collar of his overalls, yanked him backward, and swiftly drew the blade across his throat, spilling blood across the deck.

Gurney realized he had lived on Arrakis for a long time, because his first thought was not to savor victory, but to frown at the waste of viable water gurgling out of the man's severed arteries.

The attacking squad rolled forward, independent but efficient, focused on the same goal. They easily found two other workers on the engineering deck and slew them without fanfare. Gurney motioned for the team to follow him to the piloting deck.

They hammered up metal staircases, passed through bulkhead doors. One sleepy man emerged from cramped crew quarters, calling out a question more than an alarm. His mouth was still open when Orbo grabbed him by the hair, yanked his head back hard enough to snap his neck, and threw him with disgust down to the deck.

"One level up," Orbo said. "That's where we'll find the controls."

Gurney and his men ran and burst through the hatch, charging onto the piloting deck, with him and two Atreides fighters in the lead. The bulkhead door created a bottleneck, and only three could pass through at a time, but he saw instantly what he had feared.

Instead of the tiny crew Fenring had reported on the bridge, twenty armed Harkonnen soldiers faced them. Alarms had begun to ring throughout the tanker, despite their attempts at swiftness and caution.

As Orbo and two more fighters crowded through the bulkhead doorway, one of the smugglers called out, "We've been betrayed! This is too many."

"Not too many for us to fight." Gurney activated his personal shield. The other men did the same.

With a roar, Orbo pushed past them, lumbering across the deck and throwing Harkonnen fighters from side to side.

"Use your shield, man!" Gurney said.

"Don't need a shield," Orbo replied and crashed into two armed guards, grabbing them and smashing their heads together. He turned to fight two more, but they opened fire, cutting him to pieces. Lurching forward, the big smuggler managed to collapse on top of them, knocking the Harkonnens down as more Atreides fighters rushed onto the piloting deck.

The Harkonnens had advanced weapons, but Gurney's team fought like madmen. The pilot continued to work the controls, hunched over the console and glancing nervously from side to side as the battle continued around him.

"We're outnumbered, Gurney!" one of his men shouted. "But we'll fight to the death. For House Atreides!"

The others picked up the defiant cheer. "For House Atreides!"

Gurney slashed the throat of another man and glanced around the deck, looking for any additional threats. Fenring had provided a schematic of the tanker so he could see the water hold and the engineering deck. He had also noted a large escape pod on the starboard side of the bridge. He had his own plan, one his men didn't know about.

The Atreides men fought furiously. They had already lost so much with the assassination of their Duke, and now they were willing to pay with their lives for kanly, for Gurney's revenge . . . but it belonged to them as well. They had no need for regrets. So far they had killed five of the Harkonnens, losing Orbo, one other original smuggler, and two of his Atreides men.

Then the secondary door to the piloting deck opened and ten more armed Harkonnen soldiers appeared. A cry of despair rippled through his team, particularly Staban's smugglers. "This is not what we were promised!"

"We were not *promised* anything," Gurney said, "just given information we hoped would be reliable. Will you whine and snivel, or will you fight?"

"For House Atreides!" his men shouted, and their fierce response drove the Harkonnen guards back, but at the loss of more of Gurney's men. Shot in the chest, one of his men still managed to reach the pilot, shooting him through the head with a maula pistol. The pilot slumped and fell aside while the injured Atreides man shoved the bleeding body away to work the controls. The tanker lurched as Gurney's man changed their course, heading down through the rough atmosphere. Thin winds and veils of dust screeched and buffeted against the hull.

Another Harkonnen guard killed the Atreides man at the piloting controls, and the tanker careened out of control. The Harkonnens had managed to transmit a distress signal, calling for assistance, and Gurney had no doubt that Harkonnen fighters were already streaking upward from the military base in Carthag.

He didn't have enough time, and was losing too many men. They had put up enough of a fight; no one would doubt their intent. Yet the full measure of his revenge required the next step, his secret plan. "We cannot win, and I will not let us all die. To the escape pod!"

Fighting furiously, the team reacted with dismay. "I die for House of Atreides!" one of his men vowed.

"It is not necessary." Gurney ran to the starboard side of the piloting deck. "Come, all of you—to the escape pod. Join me!"

A Harkonnen guard lunged at him, and Gurney blocked him with his activated, shimmering body shield. His foe moved slowly, trying to penetrate the intangible barrier, but Gurney brought his knife into the man's gut, driving it deep, twisting, finding the abdominal artery and severing it. The man bled out within seconds, but Gurney held onto the body like another shield, backing toward the pod's hatch. He activated it with a backhanded swat. "With me! You'll die if you stay here. Harkonnen ships are coming."

"But we can't just leave!" one of his men yelled.

"We will; I command it. We've shaken them, and we'll fight elsewhere." Gurney dragged the dead Harkonnen guard, who was limp in his arms. Letting go, he fell backward into the large escape pod, and his reluctant men tumbled in after him, crowding into the interior chamber. The last ones continued to fight, and three more of Gurney's team fell . . . three more he would have to add to the verses of his sad victory song.

The water tanker roared and rattled through the atmosphere, dropping through the sky as Gurney sealed the pod, trying to stabilize the flight. Just before the escape craft disengaged, Gurney could feel the larger ship under control again. The tanker would indeed fly into Carthag as planned, its decimated, crew shaken.

Rabban would declare it a victory.

"Now!" Gurney yelled, releasing his control over the water tanker. The escape pod released, bursting out into the winds and flying to a dangerously low altitude. The clunky vessel had minimal guidance, but he hoped the Harkonnen pursuit 'thopters racing up from the industrial military city below would be more interested in saving the tanker and its valuable cargo.

Gurney controlled the pod as best he could, sending out a coded signal to Staban Tuek, asking the smugglers to intercept them wherever they crashed out in the desert. He prayed he could guide the pod close enough to the rocks to avoid being devoured by a sandworm before they could be saved. The five surviving men with him were injured and needed medical attention.

He sat hunched over his knees. The makeup covering his inkvine scar had flaked away under beads of perspiration. He thought of his sister raped and murdered by Beast Rabban, thought of Duke Leto, and dear Master Paul.

He had done this for them, and would remember that when he counted his loyal dead.

VI

In the smugglers' sietch hidden in the deep desert, the mood was a stew of somberness mixed with anger.

As the Harkonnen air defenses swooped in to intercept and escort the battered tanker, Gurney's escape pod tumbled off into the desert. Well away from the tanker, smuggler ships retrieved Gurney's pod just in time by darting into the canyons and hiding in the rock shadows as a ruthless desert storm built in the atmosphere. The Harkonnens had found the crashed escape pod, but none of the smugglers, and then the storm had driven them back to Carthag.

In the tunnels, Staban Tuek's glare was like a fusillade of weapons fire directed at Gurney. But Gurney held on to hope as if it were a lifeline. The dead had been counted after the raid, and the smugglers were dismayed at the loss of thirteen fighters, their bodies left behind in the clutches of the Harkonnen animals. Gurney was sickened by that. Of the twelve, nine loyal Atreides men had been slain and four of the original smugglers, but they'd known full well what they were fighting for; none of them would have any regrets.

He felt sadness for Orbo, even though the man had been surly and smashed Gurney's baliset, stealing music from the smuggler hideout just as smugglers stole spice from the Harkonnens. In his life, Gurney had held numerous grudges, but this was not one of them. He understood Orbo, and appreciated him now for his courage. The big man had died fighting Harkonnens, and he'd exacted his own vengeance.

Gurney only wished he could have seen the rest of the plan. . . .

"I shall write a song for them," Gurney said aloud, lost in his thoughts. "One verse for Orbo and his men, and another for the Duke's brave men. All will be remembered."

Staban's face reddened, his eyes narrowed. The smuggler leader lurched out of his alcove-cave office. "*Remembered*, Gurney Halleck? Not a one among us would forget! The raid was a failure. The Harkonnens fought better than expected." He came forward and thrust a finger in front of Gurney's face. "What I did not expect was for you to be such a coward."

"We were outnumbered and getting killed," Gurney said. "We couldn't have survived, and it took skill and courage to bring the survivors home."

"You should have fought harder, should have fought longer. We lost good men, some of my best. Thanks to you and your foolish plan, we spent half a year of profits on the spice bribe for Count Fenring and the Guild . . ." He drew a deep breath, as if he could barely phrase his own disgust. "And you lost the water! Everything! I never believed you would give up so easily. The great Gurney Halleck. I thought all your fury and passion was wrapped up in this scheme. You retreated too soon. I've heard the reports on you."

Gurney thought of the battle, of the armed Harkonnen guards on the piloting deck. "No man among us is ashamed at how he fought. We killed many. Man for man, their losses were twice ours."

"But our losses count more," Staban said. "Now I have to find more men to replace the ones we lost." The smuggler leader sounded exhausted. He shook his head as he reiterated, "And you lost all the water."

Gurney's anger boiled. He had held it inside for too long, not just about how the raid ended, but the long-simmering poison of everything that had gone wrong, the treachery since the moment that fighting first broke out on the terrible night in Arrakeen a year ago.

"I didn't want the water," he confessed in a husky voice. "I wanted revenge. I wanted kanly."

He departed, leaving Staban looking confused. Back in the escape pod he found the uniform from the last Harkonnen guard he had killed; it lay folded and cleaned as he had instructed, the knife tear in the belly repaired. He shook out the fabric, inspected it. Now he had everything he needed.

He had to get back to Carthag—and he had to hurry.

VII

The uniform fit well enough, though he despised the markings and the fact that others might look at him and consider him a Harkonnen. But the disguise was necessary. Thanks to the repressive mood that Rabban engendered among his loyal troops as well as the downtrodden people who worked the new garrison city, few people would ask questions. Gurney would use their own suspicions and fears against them. He would use Rabban against himself.

Carthag was on high alert after the attempted hijacking of the water tanker. The fact that some of the men had called out the name of House Atreides during the raid had set the Harkonnens on even more of an edge, but because the Harkonnens had won, defeating the raiders, they were giddy. Rabban had declared a day of celebration.

The water tanker had been brought in under heavy guard, and Rabban made bold announcements about how the smugglers had been thwarted, the last remnants of Atreides fighters shamefully defeated. He had mutilated the bodies of the fallen smugglers, including Gurney's men, for a macabre public spectacle. And when the people of Carthag did not cheer sufficiently, he gave orders for them to do so—and they obeyed.

The increased security bound the Harkonnen troops more tightly together in their crackdown on the city people in Carthag, and they never thought to look carefully at one another. Gurney had spent many horrible years on Giedi Prime under the Harkonnen bootheel, and he could speak convincingly to the troops, so that they easily accepted him. The Harkonnen blind spots were evident to him.

Gurney adjusted his uniform, but had removed the insignia of the tanker ship so that no one would ask questions. He couldn't stomach the other soldiers congratulating him, and none of the surviving tanker crew members were visible, even on this day of celebration.

Yes, Rabban had declared victory and publicly acknowledged the crew for their bravery in driving off the attempt. But Gurney had made subtle inquiries and was not surprised to learn that Rabban had quietly killed them, imposing punishment because they had allowed the dire situation to occur in the first place.

Gurney had known Rabban would never remain silent about the victory, about the Atreides loyalists who had been defeated. It pleased him to hear a rumor that the escape pod had crashed and all the remaining smugglers had been killed. It didn't matter how many of the people of Carthag actually believed it. Gurney was perfectly content to let Rabban think that any renegades involved were dead.

Gurney savored the anticipation as he walked confidently into the barracks, acknowledging the troops who bothered to look at him. He moved as if he had important orders from Rabban himself, and no one would challenge him. A desert hood covered his hair and the side of his face, and his stolen uniform was dust stained, some of the markings strategically obscured.

Now that the tanker was safely arrived, Rabban wanted to demonstrate largess, to show his appreciation for his troops who had been assigned to this awful planet. In the main barracks assembly hall, he had gathered his men for the event. Gurney had to see this with his own eyes. Someone had to witness his revenge, in the name of his beloved Duke Leto Atreides and all of his men who had died at the hands of the Harkonnens.

Gurney slipped from one point to another as if he had a destination, but he just wanted to keep moving, keep watching. The soldiers talked in a low buzz as they sat looking down at their trays of food. Most of the men had removed their nose plugs and face masks inside the barracks, but they still wore their desert gear. At a glance he could tell which of these soldiers had been on Arrakis for the past year and which were new arrivals.

Gurney wanted to see them all dead. They were all Harkonnens. Even the freshest arrivals were not innocent.

Rabban's very existence was like abrasive powder in Gurney's

arteries, making the center of his chest hurt. The husky man sat at
a table raised above the troops so he could look out upon the lines
of tables. Rabban had a feast set before him, far more extravagant
than the rations of his troops—but the new governor of Arrakis
had his own point to make. He did not stand as he raised a crystal
goblet in his left hand. "We have water, and on Arrakis water is
life. Our tanker arrived safely, but it was a very close thing, a near
disaster. This planet is dangerous, and there are those who wish to
harm our rule."

With his other hand he picked up a pitcher of water and poured
it into the crystal goblet. "Those who tried to steal that tanker
would steal our lives, but we stopped them." He slammed the
goblet down onto the tabletop, breaking the crystal and spilling
water . . . a stupid, wasteful thing to do on Arrakis. *We stopped
them!*" The men cheered. "This water is from the tanker we saved.
Extra rations for you on this meal, so you know your worth to
House Harkonnen."

Servants rushed in carrying pitchers, and the soldiers muttered,
but this time the buzz seemed less dour, more curious than appre-
ciative. "One cup apiece from the newly arrived supplies. Those of
you who have been with us know the very high value of the reward
I give you, the supreme value of water on Arrakis."

The soldiers grunted and cheered, and Rabban held up his crystal goblet, waiting as the servants went through the room pouring
water. Someone put another goblet on the table next to Rabban,
but he put a hand over the top, and shook his head. The servant
looked astonished. "But sir, it's . . . you don't want any water?" Rabban again refused, and the servant surreptitiously poured a goblet
for himself and gulped it down.

Into his own goblet Rabban poured a pale vintage from a green
bottle. "I will celebrate with my own reward. Caladan wine. Drink
up!" He drank deeply from the goblet, while the others consumed
their water.

Gurney had not expected this, but he didn't show any emotion,
and kept moving by the table as if he had a seat to claim or a place
to go. He stood off to one side, watching them all. Waiting.

Over the next hour Rabban consumed two bottles of Caladan

wine and demanded that the servants open a third. He got sloppy drunk, and Gurney grew impatient, nervous. Why wasn't he drinking any of the water?

It took nearly ninety minutes for the neurotoxin in the water to take effect on the others. Gurney had known it would take this long, but still felt time dilating, dragging out. He feared his presence would be discovered, and knew he needed to leave. Some of the people were noticing him, remarking on how he stood aside and was not drinking the water, not celebrating with them.

Now Rabban noticed him from his high table. His wine-bleared gaze locked onto Gurney's angry glare and seemed to see something there, recognizing an ancient memory of pain. Did Rabban even remember what he had done to Gurney's sister so long ago, the rape and murder? And what he had done to Gurney, the scarring with a whip? The inkvine scar burned on his cheek and he was sure the makeup was sloughing off. Rabban hesitated.

Suddenly, one of the soldiers groaned loudly and slumped on to the table. Others twisted and spasmed, sliding off their benches to the dusty stone floor. One after another. The Harkonnen troops inside the barracks were beset with paroxysms of pain, vomiting, twitching with their eyes rolled back in their heads. As alarms sounded, medics rushed in, but there was nothing they could do. They had all drunk the water from the tanker that Gurney had poisoned, and he knew there was no antidote. Those with a smaller body mass were affected first, while the heavier ones could only watch in horror, terrified of what was to come within the next few minutes . . . and it always came.

Rabban roused himself enough to bellow for his guards to find the perpetrator, but his protectors, too, were debilitated. Gurney watched them die, one by one and in clusters of screaming pain.

By the end of the night, hundreds of Harkonnen troops lay dead, all poisoned from the deadly nerve toxin he had poured through the sample access hatch into the tanker's cargo hold during the supposed Guild inspection. Only one taste of a droplet was a fatal dose, and Gurney had added more than a liter to the supply . . . enough to kill every man, woman and child in Carthag.

But Beast Rabban would not share the water with civilians, not with servants, not with merchants or tradesmen. He had only given it to his troops, and they were the ones condemned to death.

"Kanly?" Gurney whispered as he watched the men die, slipped out of the barracks before anyone could ask the wrong questions.

He remembered how the Harkonnens had conquered Arrakeen, not just because they'd enlisted a traitor, or because they'd been in possession of superior weapons, but also because they used archaic and unorthodox weapons, a method of attack that even Thufir Hawat had not anticipated. For the sneak attack on House Atreides, their archenemies had brought in artillery, old-fashioned projectile weapons that were normally useless due to the prevalence of shields. Many Atreides soldiers had died that night in Arrakeen and in the defensive-battery caves in the Shield Wall, bombarded by artillery projectiles.

Duke Leto had said in despair, "Their simple minds came up with a simple trick. We didn't count on simple tricks."

Now Gurney had come up with a simple retaliation of his own.

Staban Tuek, Count Fenring, and the Guild representatives had all believed that Gurney's true goal was to steal the water tanker—and that would have achieved a certain measure of revenge. The loss of that water would have placed great hardship on the Arrakis garrison and caused extreme embarrassment for Rabban.

But for Gurney, stealing the tanker—or attempting to do so—was merely a diversion. He had never intended to escape with the water because he had poisoned it while aboard the tanker. Because they'd fought so hard and lost men, the Harkonnens would never doubt that the raid was sincere. They simply hadn't had the imagination to figure out what Gurney had really been doing.

And he had known from Rabban's past behavior that he would probably attempt to buy the loyalty of his troops with a few sips of water, without knowing it was deadly poison.

All those deaths . . . Rabban would cover it up. He would make excuses to his domineering uncle, and the Baron Vladimir Harkonnen would certainly not believe them.

Gurney heaved a deep, satisfied breath, and felt a shudder—not of relief or satisfaction, but of acceptance. He had achieved *kanly*. If only Rabban himself had imbibed the poison water, his revenge would have been sweeter, but this would do for now. For Duke Leto. For young Master Paul. It was not enough, but Gurney Halleck had sent a powerful message.

Still wearing his Harkonnen disguise, Gurney slipped out of the Carthag barracks, leaving behind the moans of the dying, along with the alarms and shouting medics. Gurney struggled to conceal the satisfied smile on his face. After this massacre he would leave Carthag and return to the smugglers.

But he couldn't depart from the city just yet. He wanted to go into the town, find a merchant and spend some of the money he had brought with him. He needed to buy a new baliset, one that made sweet music to keep the smugglers company in their hideout.

Now Gurney had a new song to compose.

IMPERIAL COURT

97 years after the Battle of Corrin
and the end of the thinking machines

Nine years after the formation
of the Spacing Guild

I

Emperor Roderick Corrino was dead, and the consequences resounded through the Imperium like cracks spreading from shattered glass. The colorful Imperial court on Salusa Secundus took on a dark, frantic edge as political alliances and ambitions became frayed.

In the power vacuum, Willem Atreides guarded his long-standing position on Salusa Secundus, mentored by Roderick himself. Though the young man had proved his worth and abilities countless times, he knew that simple competence might not be enough for the vital position that had become vacant—as court chamberlain. He would have to make his case.

Willem knew he was the most qualified and dedicated person for the job, but others would be scheming and distorting, jockeying for position to empower their noble families, thinking of themselves first and the Imperium second. Such thoughts made lines of concern appear on his brow.

Standing now inside the bustling kaleidoscope of the throne room, he waited for his meeting with young Emperor Javicco, twenty-three years old, the only son of Roderick.

Although Willem had served at court for almost a decade, placed there as a special boon to his famous ancestor Vorian Atreides, Willem had not married nor had any children. He was thirty, still relatively young among the powerful nobles here, and he had time to build his bloodline. Oh, Willem had other Atreides cousins in a different, distant branch of the family, but as far as he could tell they had no grand ambitions.

Even though he was well connected, he'd been feeling very much alone in the palace.

An intelligent, dedicated man, Willem was known to focus on his work even-handedly, which his mentor, Emperor Roderick, had appreciated, and Vorian had counseled. Now, Willem vowed to serve the unsteady new Emperor—if only he got the chance.

Javicco summoned him at last. Criers called out his name even though Willem stood plainly there with other finely dressed courtiers in the grand hall. Other ambitious people looked up at him, some with envy, some with hungry eyes. Many of them wanted the influential position to which he aspired.

Under prismatic skylights, he walked past the cool mist of a rainbow fountain, approaching the throne on its dais, which had formerly held Roderick Corrino. Willem bowed respectfully before the young Emperor.

After Roderick Corrino's sudden death, rumors, accusations, and confusion had swept across the Imperium like a cold squall on Caladan, where Willem had grown up with his younger brother Orry. The newly crowned Javicco needed a chamberlain, a key person who managed, influenced, and controlled the court, interacted with the Council of Nobles, the ambassadors, and ministers.

The previous chamberlain, a man named Lopar, had fled under mysterious circumstances. Some said that Lopar had rushed away because he was complicit in the death of the Emperor, while others believed he had fled for his life before he could be made into a scapegoat.

Now, almost a century after the fall of Omnius in the Battle of Corrin, most of humanity was at last united except for a few groups of worlds. Willem had studied the enormous puzzle of the Imperium for years, and he thought he understood it. It was his mission to help Javicco rule as best he could.

In the crowded receiving room, the Emperor rose from his throne and said to him, "Follow me into my antechamber, where we can talk away from all this noise. My other business of today is concluded." Willem could see that Javicco wanted a break from the crushing new responsibilities he faced daily.

The Emperor's lavish withdrawing chamber was the size of the house where Willem had grown up on Caladan. More cool fountains filled the air with soothing noises, and numerous green plants and blooming flowers made the place a sanctuary.

Javicco dropped down onto a divan filled with cushions, but instead of lounging back into the decadence, he sat tense, as if all the pillows and colorful hangings in the world could not relax him. He looked up with an uncertain smile. "So, I am told you wish to be my new chamberlain."

Willem stood straight and confident as he presented himself. "If you please, Sire. I will serve in whatever way the Imperium can best use me." He bowed, then raised his gaze to look directly into Javicco's eyes. He saw a hint of a hunted animal there. "For nine years here I have demonstrated my loyalty and my abilities, and I believe I am qualified and best suited for this vital job. If given the opportunity, I would always advise you wisely and faithfully."

Javicco frowned, as if disappointed in what Willem had just said. He patted the cushion next to him. "Sit beside me so we can talk like normal people. My life was hard enough before as Crown Prince. Now it is almost impossible."

Willem took the seat beside him, hoping he had not done anything wrong. "I trust you are not displeased by my directness, Sire?"

Javicco sighed. "As the able representative of House Atreides, you only said what they all say. I've heard the same enthusiastic auditions from House Bastin, House Mbangwe, House Auradia, and House Harkonnen."

The last name gave Willem a cold chill. For years at court, he had kept his distance from Danvis Harkonnen, the great grandson of the notorious jihad coward Abulurd Harkonnen, who had nearly lost the human race at Corrin. In recent years, though, Danvis had risen to prominence at court.

Everyone knew of the rivalry between the two Houses. Willem frowned bitterly as the operative word crossed his mind. *Rivalry?* More like a blood feud. Danvis's sister Tula had tricked and seduced his beloved brother Orry, murdering him on their wedding night. No Atreides could ever forgive that.

"I am different from the others," he said.

"And why is that?"

"Because I mean what I say, as a matter of personal and family honor."

Finally the young Emperor chuckled and offered Willem a glass of purple wine. One of the servants who'd been hovering in the doorway of the withdrawing room came forward with the decanter, pouring first for the guest and then for the Emperor.

Sitting beside Javicco, Willem sipped his wine, aware that it was one of the most expensive vintages on a thousand planets, but the taste in his mouth had gone flat. "I will not push you, Sire. You know the selfless work I have done. You know I am not scheming to build up my family name. I have no secret agenda—only your agenda. Your father trusted me."

Javicco took a gulp of the wine, then hung his head. He looked very young and lost. "My father trusted you, but that doesn't mean I automatically have the same feelings toward you. You have to earn it."

Willem knew the young man spoke the truth. "And I will earn it, if you give me the chance."

"My mother was one of my father's most trusted advisers," Javicco mused, "and she gave him wise counsel throughout their marriage. Alas, she can't serve the same role for me. His death affected her even more than it did me, and she has withdrawn to our private estate in the west, shunning Imperial affairs. My two sisters are married off with powerful noblemen, and they will pull strings to help build the influence of their new families."

Willem said carefully, "I would never seek to countermand your sisters, Sire."

Javicco brushed him aside. "I never listen to Tikya and Wissoma anyway. The only one I really liked was little Nantha, but she was murdered by a Butlerian mob long ago."

Realizing that he had unsettled Willem, the young Emperor set his wine aside and stood up from the colorful divan. "I am harried on all sides by ambitious people who claim they will serve me selflessly. Your application has been heard, Willem Atreides, and I know your qualifications. I will consider you carefully for the role, just as I will consider the others." Javicco looked hard at him. "Including Danvis Harkonnen."

II

When the Potentate of the Arua Confederation arrived at Salusa Secundus, he came with enough pageantry to suggest that his group of unallied planets wielded as much power as the Corrino Imperium.

The Potentate's entourage was indeed impressive, Danvis Harkonnen thought. Curious, he followed the newly landed group of dignitaries and ambassadors, accessible and ready to welcome these important guests. He would help them navigate the accepted protocol in Emperor Javicco's presence. For political reasons, it was wise to act as if he were their friend.

As a show of respect, Imperial honor guards marched out of the towering palace gates, flowing in perfect lines and holding the Golden Lion banners of House Corrino to greet the visitors. In previous years, the Potentate of Arua had developed a proposal for unification, but Emperor Roderick had never made the necessary concessions for a proper alliance. Now that the former Emperor was dead, his son Javicco might be an entirely different story.

Moving smoothly, as if he were an important escort, Danvis walked near the front of the visitors. He wore an embellished purple cape and high, polished boots. The finery was uncomfortable but necessary. At times Danvis missed the loose woolen garb designed for the wet winter storms of Lankiveil . . . but as representative of House Harkonnen, he had lived in the Imperial capital for several years now. By making himself indispensable at court, Danvis sought to secure his family's prominence after so many years of disgrace.

His older sister Valya, the Mother Superior of the mysterious Sisterhood, had given him his orders when he'd first arrived here, wide-eyed but ready to do what was necessary. Valya's allegiance had to be balanced between her family name and the Sisterhood, but she had instructed him in how to become a true power broker at court. And Danvis had done so for nine years. He knew what to do.

"This way, my Lord Potentate," Danvis said with a welcoming smile as he invited the visitors into the palace. "I am not certain how to address you?" Javicco certainly had protocol ministers to handle such subtleties, but Danvis had gotten here first.

The Potentate was a round-faced man with fleshy folds around his eyes, a gray mustache, and a narrow beard that emerged from his chin like a squirt of curly hair. He turned a hard gaze toward Danvis. "You may call me Excellency, or Your Supreme Majesty."

Danvis hesitated. "I acknowledge your power, sir, although here in the court on Salusa, the latter title might be confused with that of our Emperor."

The Potentate gave him a surprised look, then smiled stiffly. "Your point is accepted. As for you, I admire a man with the courage to speak up."

The young man gave a cordial bow. "Please feel free to consult me if you have any questions. I am Danvis, the head of House Harkonnen."

Beside the Potentate walked a confident woman with dark hair, soft cheekbones, and a small mouth stained crimson. Wispy veils covered her hair, neck, and left cheek, but they intrigued more than obscured. From her demeanor Danvis sensed that this woman used her beauty like a seductive weapon. He realized that she was the person to impress, ultimately the wielder of influence. This was Krissanda, daughter of the Potentate.

He had heard rumors that the Potentate of Arua, or more likely Krissanda, might have had something to do with Roderick's death, removing him in favor of a more pliable Javicco. To anyone else, Danvis would never assert that, but privately—if it happened to be true—he might find their ambitions useful, depending on the outcome of negotiations.

"We are charmed to make your acquaintance, Danvis Harkonnen," Krissanda said in a voice that said exactly the opposite. Her eyes—a very dark brown, or perhaps black?—flashed. "Father, did we come here to see a minor lordling, or Emperor Javicco himself?"

The Potentate touched his forehead with a finger, a symbolic gesture. "Of course, my dear. Priorities. I know you want to have a look at the young Emperor. And as for you, Danvis Harkonnen, please facilitate our meeting with him, and we will be in your debt."

Danvis was already moving, brushing aside the annoyed-looking protocol ministers and courtiers who had finally arrived. Taking charge, Danvis led the Arua entourage into the vast receiving hall. He shouted out, "Emperor Javicco Corrino! Fifth Emperor of humanity since the fall of the hated thinking machines! I present a most honored guest, the Potentate of Arua." He raised his hands in a grandiose gesture, then bowed and stepped aside.

The Potentate's bodyguards stood like a wall in their loose, flowing garments over ornamental, but visible, body armor. Imperial sentinels stood along the walls, ready to defend Emperor Javicco against any attack, but Danvis sensed no inordinate tension in the air, just a display of human plumage.

The young Emperor was sitting on his throne, adjusting his legs to find a comfortable position. Obviously, he had rushed there to receive the visitors. Javicco rose half to his feet, reconsidered, and sat back down. As the Potentate and his beautiful daughter marched forward in front of the thunder of footsteps from his many retainers, Javicco decided to stand after all. "Welcome, esteemed Potentate. I am pleased to greet such honored guests."

In the flurry of people, costumes, and banners, as well as the ministers who came forward, Danvis found himself pushed to the sidelines. No matter, he had made his mark and drawn the attention he wanted.

The Potentate stepped forward without bowing and spoke in a booming voice, "I have returned, Imperial Majesty Javicco Corrino. I express my sympathy for the tragic loss of your father and also congratulations for the beginning of your own illustrious reign. May you rule with wisdom and foresight to help humanity thrive, after so many centuries of tribulations."

"Yes . . . my noble compatriot." Fumbling for a proper title to use, Javicco looked toward his protocol ministers, who stood too far away. "We have had enough tribulations. It is time to bring together the human race so that we never let a nightmare like the thinking machines occur again."

Mutters of agreement ran through the crowded throne room. Someone shouted, "Hear, hear!"

Thinking quickly, Danvis shouted out the same, and soon it became a resonating chant. "Hear, hear!"

When the commotion finally died down, Javicco resumed his seat on the great chair. Danvis considered hurrying forward to advise him, but the Potentate said in a loud voice, his words causing a hush as if an axe blade had swept across the crowd. "And the best way to strengthen the factions of humanity . . ." He placed a hand on Krissanda's shoulder as if stroking a prized possession. "Is with a marriage alliance!"

The young woman coyly rearranged her gossamer veils, not revealing more of her face, but somehow inspiring a greater enticement.

During the swiftly arranged welcome reception afterward, servants strolled through the crowd bearing trays with fine wines, strong liqueurs, iced juices, and other drinks. Danvis selected a fluted glass of pink poma juice, a strong and bitter extract reputed to have healthy properties. For most, it was an acquired taste, but Danvis had always enjoyed it. He quaffed the drink and set the empty glass on the next tray that went by.

Wheels turned in his mind, and he knew he had to go speak with his influential cousin as soon as possible.

III

Willem Atreides already had important work to do at court, whether or not he was selected as the new chamberlain. He served on several Landsraad committees, acted as trade spokesperson among consortiums of worlds. He had paperwork to study and decisions to make, and he preferred to ponder alone.

Now, knowing his rivals for the important court position, he reviewed their backgrounds, strengths, and weaknesses. He looked into the family histories and finances of Houses Bastin, Mbangwe, and Auradia. He already knew the despicable history of House Harkonnen.

Willem knew that the other candidates were surely investigating him and the Atreides line, but rather than relying solely on their merits, he suspected they would also play political games, trying to distort records and besmirch his name. Let them try. Willem would not stoop to that level. He was no desperate climber seeking political clout. Emperor Roderick had known his competence, and Javicco would soon understand it as well.

After a polite knock, his executive assistant interrupted him, peeping through the door. The middle-aged man's narrow face was flushed, his pale eyes averted. His words were filled with apologies—as always. Willem had scolded the man for being too obsequious, for couching even the simplest phrases in soft terms, but his behavior seemed unchangeable. "I apologize, my Lord. This interruption is inexcusable, I know, but you have visitors. I am so sorry to disrupt your work."

Willem knew the constant interruptions would only grow worse if he were appointed the official chamberlain, but he still wanted the position. Quelling a sigh, he set aside the dossiers of the other contenders and sat up to receive visitors. "Let them in. I'm sure it's important."

"Yes, my Lord—important by its very nature." The nervous assistant raised his chin. "They say they are Atreides."

Curiosity and confusion warred within Willem's mind as he rose to his feet. He had few relatives left on Caladan after Tula Harkonnen had murdered Orry. But some distant cousins likely claimed Atreides blood, and no doubt more would appear out of the woodwork once he became chamberlain.

Before the assistant could step away, a broad-shouldered man pushed his way into Willem's office. He wore an ornamented leather vest over a clean long-sleeved white shirt. His long hair had been brushed and tied back in a green and black ribbon, though the remaining kinks and unruliness suggested that brushing was not its normal state. His beard was even less under control, but his warm grin showed sincere good humor.

"Willem Atreides! You have done well for yourself . . . and for our name. It is long past time that the branches of our family come together."

Out of habit, Willem extended the half-handshake of the Imperium. "You have me at a disadvantage. And who are you? A cousin?"

"A half-cousin." The man laughed. "Though in a dispersed family, I would not split hairs. I am Luc Atreides from Kepler, home to some of the children sired by our mutual ancestor Vorian Atreides." He engulfed Willem's hand in his large grip.

From behind, others pushed past Luc. The executive assistant did his best to hold them back, but the other Atreides family members ignored him, eager to meet Willem. He was introduced to six similarly dressed young men and women, including one woman with experience as a field medic, but Luc was proudest to introduce an intelligent and energetic eight-year-old boy, his son Ranny. Luc and his companions wore their best garments, though nothing like Imperial court finery.

Despite his initial skepticism about "long-lost family members," Willem was glad to meet them. He knew full well that Vorian— who was centuries old thanks to a life-extension treatment—had sired many children from other wives and lovers. Vorian had lived on Caladan for many years, fell in love, produced a family, and then watched his wife and even his children grow old. He finally left, wandered, and settled down to a new obscure life on Kepler, where he fell in love with another woman, Mariella, who bore him more children. He had lived with Mariella for decades until he was forced to leave by Emperor Salvador, Roderick's brother.

"We'll have many stories to share," Willem said, then called out to his assistant, "Arrange for a large banquet, so we can welcome my new cousins to the Imperial fold."

Even if Luc and his companions had conveniently appeared at a time when Willem's political power was about to surge, he realized he might need allies at court, as well as an expanded noble family. He felt glad to know he was no longer alone.

"A banquet!" Luc clapped him on the back. "I guarantee that we're hungry, though your fancy foods may be too rich for us."

Young Ranny stepped forward. "But I'll try them. I want to experience things."

Luc laughed even louder. "Listen to the boy. He'll be going places! Oh, and we also brought some gifts from Kepler, including buriak fruit and gornet meat. We shall share, and make it a real feast."

IV

A large, comfortable estate on the outskirts of the palace grounds, the Harkonnen Consulate was secluded on private diplomatic territory, surrounded by tall, impenetrable hedges. Although Danvis, and all the important noble families, also had lavish quarters inside the enormous palace, the Consulate was a sanctuary against unwanted observers.

Having been coached by Valya, his powerful elder sister, Danvis knew his duties, and by now he could play the game of Imperial intrigues by instinct. He remained visible at court, spent his days presenting motions, looking prominent, making himself memorable. There was a large, political advantage to being seen and noticed, Danvis knew.

But there was just as great a reward in being completely invisible.

His younger cousin, Gerhard, served as a formal emissary of the noble family, though he reported to Danvis. Gerhard remained out of sight most of the time at the Consulate, and he had a knack for acquiring information and accomplishing missions quietly. Following his own interests and obsessions, the young man had used Harkonnen diplomatic funds to build an extravagant addition to the consulate house, a conservatory where he tended his collection of rare insect and arachnid specimens.

Now, busy with what he had learned, Danvis searched for his cousin inside the large plaz-and-metal structure, intent on briefing him. In the humid moistness, ferns and flowering bushes thrived. The air was aflutter with colorful butterfly wings, and dragonflies buzzed past like attack ships. Iridescent beetles crawled up stems and trunks.

As he hurried forward, Danvis heard a crunch under his boot

and saw that he had just crushed one of the specimens. A metaphor for the Imperium, he thought. No matter how gaudy and beautiful a person tried to be, he might still be unnoticed and crushed if he got in the way.

He found Gerhard standing in front of a silvery web that spanned two meters, a tapestry of spider silk strung from twig to twig, extending into a complex pattern. Small red spiders danced up and down the lines, hatchlings from an egg sac that had opened a week ago and now the creatures were as long as a thumb.

Gerhard was a lean young man, except for his rounded paunch, and he had bristly silver hair with streaks of dyed blue, an affectation some said, but he said he didn't care what people thought. Humming to himself, he touched the web as if plucking a harp string, which attracted the spiders. Several scuttled onto his hand, which he withdrew from the web and then watched with fascination while the red spiders circled his fingers, crawled down his palm, and ran around his wrist. He reached out to another part of the web, touched the string, and let the spiders run back to their safe lines.

Danvis said nothing as he observed. After the spiders had crawled from Gerhard's hand, he said, "Aren't those poisonous?"

"Somewhat, but not aggressive. I might get a welt if one bit me, but I'd need to harass them before that happened. Instead, I am coaxing them." The young man raised his eyebrows. "Even dangerous things can be coaxed."

"You are learning," Danvis said with a smile. "That's exactly what we need to talk about. Emperor Roderick's death provides numerous opportunities for us to empower House Harkonnen."

Gerhard looked bored. "That much has been obvious for months." A dragonfly hovered in front of Danvis's face as if measuring him as prey, then darted off.

Danvis continued, "In the initial turmoil, all the noble families were just trying to protect what they had, but now it is time for House Harkonnen to take another step forward. I've already spoken to Javicco, planted the seed. He needs a new court chamberlain, who will be the most powerful political figure in the palace. After Lopar fled, Javicco has avoided filling the position." He clicked his tongue against his teeth. "The young Emperor shows signs of paranoia. He doesn't know whom he can trust. I should be the new chamberlain. It would raise our family's power, wealth, and respect."

"Respect . . ." Gerhard turned back to watch the spiders moving on their expansive web. "It's about time we had respect, after our family was exiled to Lankiveil, and our great-grandfather had to hide in shame. Our whole family should not be blamed for the cowardice of one man! The disgrace was caused by the Atreides."

Danvis glowered at his cousin. "Yes, we loathe the Atreides, to the very last one of them. Vorian Atreides ruined Abulurd Harkonnen—and us. If one of us were to become chamberlain, though, history would forget any missteps in the past."

Distracted by his insect pets, Gerhard wandered through the conservatory, holding out his hands while butterflies swirled around him. A large predator moth swooped in, breaking the serene moment as it snatched a jewel-green butterfly out of the air and crunched its head while flapping away.

Gerhard smiled. "If you are the best candidate for the job, you will be chosen."

"I must be chosen, regardless. Several others have applied, but they are weak and too obviously ambitious. Mbangwe, Auradia, Bastin. More importantly, we must prevent an Atreides from filling that position."

Gerhard paused in front of a plaz-walled display case. Inside, a large nest like a pockmarked moon hung from a dead branch. Black-winged hornets swooped around, and when Gerhard approached the transparent barrier, the insects responded to the movement. They flashed toward him like angry projectiles. Their wings hummed furiously, and their mandibles clacked against the plaz. Their stingers battered like spears. Even though they could not break through, the hornets kept attacking.

"These lovely onyx hornets are far more poisonous than the red spiders," Gerhard said, "Far more aggressive."

Danvis smiled. "Maybe we should unleash a few of them in the private quarters of our noble rivals. Poison our foes and remove them from consideration."

His cousin chuckled. "That would work, of course, but if several of your rivals conveniently died from the poisonous sting of an onyx hornet? The welt would be found, the poison identified . . . and it would be traced to me. Though only a few people know of my collection, I might still be found out." He shook his head. "No, we need to find an alternative that is not so obvious." Despite being his superior, Danvis had to hurry to follow the younger man. "I have a better suggestion."

Gerhard squinted through the transparent barrier of another enclosure. On the other side, dozens of blooming poppies rose up, red flowers whose intense colors were like a shout against the eyes.

"Flowers?" Danvis asked.

"Not the flowers, cousin. Watch closely."

After a moment, Danvis saw a rippled blur in the air—a cloud of small buzzing specks no larger than the head of a pin. Though the swarm contained thousands, he could barely see them.

"A nasty cloud of inigo gnats," Gerhard explained. "Barely visible, short-lived. They are quite rare and exotic, and no one knows I have them. I obtained them from a special broker in the jungles of Rossak, going through a series of middlemen who also met unfortunate deaths afterward."

Danvis mused as he looked into the enclosure. "But why are they so interesting, and why have you gone to all that trouble to get them?"

Gerhard chuckled. "Not just interesting, cousin—they are toxic, and no one knows I have them. Deadly toxic. Even a small sample cloud, if released in the presence of a target, would bite and poison him fatally. They would then fly away and die, never to be noticed. The slightest breeze would whisk away their miniature husks. And within an hour or two, the victim would perish. No one would ever know the source of the poison. It would appear to be a mere skin rash."

"Gnats . . ." Danvis said, reminded of House Harkonnen in the early years. "One should never underestimate the deadly power of a seemingly small and insignificant thing."

Gerhard looked at him. "Do you like my suggestion, then?"

With a nod, Danvis gave the go-ahead.

"I will collect samples, and we can decide how best to distribute them to our rivals."

V

Willem and his newfound cousins consumed an extravagant evening banquet on a well-lit open balcony under the bright lights of the Salusan capital. Luc Atreides sat next to Willem at the head of the table, while the rest of the Kepler Atreides spread out on either side. Various dishes were arrayed in front of them, considered the Imperium's finest, ten times the amount of food that even a starving group could have eaten. Any dish that wasn't to their liking was simply passed along in favor of the next recipe.

The casual conversation and spontaneous laughter made Willem think of a normal family meal. Although the palace attendants were nonplussed that the forms were not followed, that the proper napkins, chargers, drinking vessels and utensils were not used in the appropriate fashion, Willem didn't mind at all. This group cared little for the restrictions and expectations of court life. Seeing them, Willem thought of a Caladan reference—fish out of water.

Nevertheless, the people easily fell into telling stories about Vorian Atreides, the legendary, ageless man who had appeared as an unexpected mentor for Willem and Orry on Caladan.

"I was there when Vorian died," Willem said, feeling the sting of pain and sadness, and realizing everyone was listening. "It was in the ruins of Corrin under the red-giant sun. Valya Harkonnen came to kill him. They dueled, and Vorian defeated her, but you know how treacherous Harkonnens are." Around the table the Kepler cousins looked sickened. "Even though Vorian resolved the feud and let her live afterward, Valya had planted a bomb on his ship. It blew up in midair. We all watched him die." Acid filled his voice.

Luc hung his head. "Assassins came to Kepler hunting for Vorian, too. They . . . they burned the farmhouse, killed our grandmother Mariella." The big man grumbled. "Vorian had a habit of bringing tragedy wherever he went."

Willem sat up straighter. "Don't blame him for the hateful things others did. My vengeance is directed toward the Harkonnens, where it belongs."

Luc nodded solemnly and said, " I suppose you are right. We needed to hear wisdom from our cousin."

The meal went on, and finally Willem broached an important subject. "Luc, you've come here at an uncertain time. After Emperor Roderick's death, many families are jockeying for power. Have you come here wanting positions at court? Is that what you think I can do for you?"

The conversation around the table fell into a hushed, uncomfortable silence. Luc Atreides finally laughed out loud, and he gestured toward the view of the towering city buildings, the dazzling display of lights. "For this? What in the world would we do here?"

Willem frowned. "Then why did you come?"

Luc quaffed his drink. "With so much happening on Salusa Secundus, we knew that you had no family here, no real noble obligations. So we came to invite you back to Kepler."

Now it was Willem's turn to be surprised. "To visit, you mean?"

"No, to live there! With all your cousins and second cousins and . . . whatever the hell they're called on a family tree. We're all still Atreides. Leave this Imperial Court, stay with us at first if you like, and we hope you eventually settle down for the rest of your life. Enjoy yourself for a change! Why would you want to be here?"

Willem liked the idea of getting to know his extended family, and was relieved that these other Atreides weren't just seeking personal glory. "Because I might be selected as Emperor Javicco's new chamberlain, and then I will have responsibilities for the Imperium. If that happens, my days of leisure traveling will be over. We must wait and see what the new Emperor decides."

VI

The Imperial summons was curt and businesslike, with a stern warning against delay. As Willem read the note from the stony-faced courier, he frowned in puzzlement. "Of course I will come. When have I ever ignored a request from the Emperor?"

The courier seemed cold and angry—toward him specifically. "Be sure that you do not ignore this one. It is not a *request*."

Reading the formal declaration again, Willem got the sense that Javicco was upset with him. He wondered what had happened.

He had arranged for Luc Atreides and his party to be shown around the capital for the day, while he spent the afternoon tending to administrative duties. Now, as Willem rushed through the palace corridors, many courtiers and clerks fell ominously quiet as he strode past, casting sidelong glances at him. He heard surprise and indignation in their whispered words. Disturbingly, someone muttered "assassin," and "poison."

Willem increased his pace, determined to speak privately with the young Emperor. Arriving in the throne room, he expected to be ushered into the withdrawing chamber for a quiet discussion, as before, but he immediately saw this was different.

The large hall was filled with concerned, muttering people, and he sensed a distinctly different tenor from the usual energetic bustle. Honor guards cleared the way, leaving an open path—a dangerous gauntlet?—for Willem to pass through, and the voices fell into a hush around him.

Glancing to one side, he saw Danvis Harkonnen standing haughty and aloof, almost staring through him, as if Willem were not there—or soon would not be there. His pulse increased. Just seeing his hated enemy made bitterness swell within him.

Javicco sat on the Golden Lion throne, looking small on the enormous block of Hagal crystal. In the months since his father's abrupt death, Javicco had struggled to keep the Imperium moving forward, but it was like a boat crashing through whitewater rapids. The young man had been forced to accept so much sudden responsibility that he'd never been given time to properly grieve the death of his father. His sisters must also be mourning, but they offered no real support for him. Although Tikya and Wissoma had come back to Salusa Secundus for their father's grand funeral, they'd since gone home to their lavish estates with their noble husbands. Their mother Haditha had withdrawn to her private, isolated estate.

Right now, Javicco definitely needed people he could trust. He needed honest advice from a worthy chamberlain. And from the mood in the room, Willem thought that someone—Danvis Harkonnen, maybe?—had been trying to stain the honor of House Atreides, which would explain the strange atmosphere in the large chamber.

As Willem approached the throne, the muttering grew louder, and he heard the word "assassin" whispered again. But he had done nothing wrong, and needed to show it. Determined, he stopped at the base of the dais and bowed deeply, then stood straight and proud. "You summoned me, Sire."

Javicco wore a sickened, disbelieving expression. "I called you because I demand an explanation." His voice wavered, but beneath his uncertainty was anger and surprise.

Willem faced the young man with a steady gaze and demeanor, ignoring everyone else in the throne room. "I will give you honest and objective answers, as always, Sire. My goal is only to strengthen the Imperium and my Emperor."

"And that is why you insisted so stridently that I choose you as my next chamberlain?" Javicco demanded.

Willem blinked at the sharp vitriol, but kept himself calm. "I made an objective case on my own behalf, I hope, and you will decide whether or not it is a convincing one. I trust your judgment, Sire. I know several other names have been presented to you."

"I no longer have several names!" Javicco said. "Not anymore! This morning, the best candidates from House Auradia, Bastin, and

Mbangwe were found dead in their quarters. All three of them—killed by some insidious and unknown poison."

Willem's mouth opened, but he could find no response. "I . . . I knew nothing of this, Sire."

Danvis Harkonnen muttered in a loud stage whisper. "Of course you would say that."

"A red rash was found on the exposed skin of each victim, some kind of contact poison, a deadly toxin. It struck them down so quickly they had no chance to call out for help."

"My condolences to their noble families," Willem said, then squared his shoulders. "Am I accused of having something to do with this heinous crime? I'm an Atreides. I succeed through competence, not treachery."

"Three dead nobles would disagree," Danvis muttered loudly enough for all to hear.

"A green-and-black ribbon was found tied near each body" Javicco said in an accusing tone. "Are those not Atreides colors?"

Again, Willem forced himself not to lash out. "Green and black appear in infinite places, Sire. I swear I had nothing to do with this treacherous act. All last evening I hosted a banquet for my family members who arrived from off planet. Numerous witnesses can verify this."

"Maybe these Atreides cousins came with an off-world poison," Danvis said, and the muttering in the throne room rose to a din.

Emperor Javicco let the noise ripple out for long moments before he raised his hand for quiet. "The fact remains that three rivals for the position you covet have been eliminated. Of the original list of finalists, only you and Danvis Harkonnen remain."

Willem flashed a glare toward his archenemy, but Danvis simply stood cool and competent. The Atreides nobleman turned back to the Golden Lion Throne. "I'm certain House Harkonnen could easily find any number of markets where green and black ribbons could be purchased."

He bowed and withdrew from the Emperor.

VII

I t truly is the perfect plan, cousin," said Gerhard, his eyes shining.
Danvis listened as the intense young man explained with
animated gestures as he provided details. The two sat in a private
dining room in the Harkonnen Consulate, finishing a meal of roast
newborn vealpups.

His cousin was normally a quiet and reserved person, and his
eyes showed the swift calculations churning beneath the surface.
Listening to him now, Danvis was surprised by his uncharacteristic
energy and ambition.

"Our secondary rivals are already out of the way—Bastin, Auradia, Mbangwe," Danvis said. "Your nasty little gnats poisoned them.
The toxin remains unidentified, and the shadow of suspicion has
fallen entirely on Willem Atreides." He sipped a fresh, cool glass
of poma juice, rolling the taste around in his mouth. "Now all that
remains is him and me—as it should be." He wiped his lips.

"We shall seal it by destroying the Atreides," Gerhard said. "The,
ah, icing on the cake, to use a colloquialism." His cousin leaned
forward at the table, pushing aside the vealpup carcass and leaving
only bones and moist ribbons of fat. "And here is what we must do.
You yourself will become the next victim. Willem Atreides is already the prime suspect, and when they find your body struck down
by the same toxin, there will be no doubt. House Atreides will be
utterly ruined."

Danvis almost choked in alarm. "That is a ridiculous plan. I wish
to promote our family, but not to the extent of killing myself. That
would leave you in charge of House Harkonnen."

Gerhard seemed darkly amused. "Trust me, the plan is far more
complex than that. Although inigo toxin is not well studied, the

chemistry has been sufficiently identified that I can synthesize a viable preemptive antidote. You have nothing to worry about."

Danvis twisted loose a rib bone the size of his forefinger. He nibbled on the tender, flavorful meat as he considered. "You want me to expose myself to a swarm of your deadly gnats? Intentionally?"

"You will fall into a deathlike coma, but you will recover—and not until Willem Atreides has been blamed, stripped of his power and holdings . . . maybe even executed, if we are lucky." Gerhard dabbed at his mouth with a napkin. "It has to be convincing. When you collapse, seemingly dead, no one will doubt that Willem Atreides struck you down just as he did the others." His grin widened. "You will appear to be the victim, the martyr, and surely Emperor Javicco will reward us and destroy House Atreides." Almost as an afterthought, he said, "I promise I can awaken you at the appropriate time."

Danvis remained uneasy, but gradually he nodded as the pieces of the plan began to fit together. He tossed aside the stripped rib bone and took another sip of his tart juice. "If you are so confident in this antidote, then why don't you become the victim? I could act outraged, declare kanly on House Atreides."

"Come now, cousin! No one cares about me. Few even notice me at court, because you are the most powerful and visible representative of our family. I am not a candidate for the job Willem wants, but you are."

Danvis knew the other man was right. Though they hadn't yet received the dessert course, he rose from the table. "Let us take care of this before some other unexpected crisis throws Javicco into an uproar."

IN A PRIVATE wing of the Consulate residence, Gerhard had built a small laboratory adjacent to the insect conservatory. When Danvis saw the preparations ready and waiting, he knew that his cousin had been planning this all along. "You knew what I would decide," he accused.

Gerhard raised his eyebrows, aloof. "I simply wanted to run experiments before I raised the possibility. I believe I have the proper formulation now."

Over the next hour, the younger man monitored Danvis's metabolism in order to calculate the precise dosage. Gerhard hummed confidently as he worked. "Not much room for error. The toxin must affect you sufficiently that you appear to be dead. Your life signs almost undetectable."

Both men smiled at each other, and Danvis sighed. "And then I will awaken into a new world for House Harkonnen."

Without warning, Gerhard jabbed him with the inoculator. "There, the antidote will be at its full effect in an hour."

Danvis winced, rubbing his arm. "I should go to my palace offices, somewhere I can be easily found after you release the gnats. Then we will set the wheels in motion." He added in a quiet voice, trying not to sound afraid. "The inigo toxin . . . will it hurt?"

"Of course not," his cousin said, too quickly.

"You don't know at all, do you?"

The other man just shrugged.

"You can arrange to have the gnats discreetly released into my offices."

Gerhard said, "Leave that to me. As always."

BACK IN THE palace, with his executive assistant guarding against unwanted visitors, Danvis attended to a backlog of ministerial work. He submitted an amended application for the office of chamberlain. With the loss of the other three candidates, as well as the uncertainty surrounding the "unreliable" Willem Atreides, Danvis wrote a convincing argument that he was the clear choice for such an important role.

Outside in the lavish halls of government, colorfully dressed nobles and diplomats moved about, preoccupied with their urgent business. Danvis reviewed the minutes from the last full session of the Council of Nobles . . . but to him it all seemed like so much dithering. Once he was chamberlain, he would make sure that the Imperium focused on vital activities, and even, he thought as he remembered the ambitions of the Potentate of Arua, the consolidation of the entire human race.

Danvis ran his fingers along the surface of his desk. It was not an ancient piece of furniture, but rather new and modern, reflecting how House Harkonnen had risen from disgrace and exile on Lankiveil. Yes, he thought, his generation would bring about a renaissance . . . and this new scheme was an important step.

Hearing a thin whine, he looked up to see a tiny blur near the air vent, little specks that swirled around, insects so small they were little more than vapor. He heard the buzzing come closer, then felt the prickle of a thousand tiny needles. . . .

VIII

When shouts of dismay rang through the administrative wing of Javicco's palace, Willem rushed to see what else had gone wrong. He was hyper-alert now, and suspicious.

He had just finished conversation and strong coffee with Luc Atreides. Although the other Kepler Atreides had gone to discuss possible trade deals for their home planet, Luc brought his young son Ranny with him as an educational experience.

Hearing the shouts, the three of them ran together to investigate, following the source of the noise. They reached the designated Harkonnen offices and saw a pale, shocked executive assistant waiting in the hall. The man stared at his hands as if something had been snatched away from him.

A uniformed doctor from the Suk school led the way, emerging from the inner office and shaking his head as two attendants carried out a body—the body of Danvis Harkonnen! The gray-faced man lay sprawled on a suspensor stretcher with his eyes closed, one arm dangling over the side. A bright red rash covered his neck, face, and hands. Danvis's face was twisted in a rictus of pain. He didn't move.

Emotions boiled up inside Willem as he stared. For much of his life, he had wanted to see his rival dead. Young Ranny stared at the body as it was carried past, his eyes glinting like those of a hungry predator.

Luc Atreides grumbled loudly enough for everyone to hear. "I've long wanted to see every Harkonnen gone for all the agony they caused House Atreides. I hope he suffered a great deal."

Willem squeezed shut his burning eyes, which only sharpened the memories of his sweet brother Orry, slaughtered in the wedding bed after Danvis's sister had seduced him. She must have taken vicious joy in slashing Orry's throat at the moment he thought he was happy. Willem and Vorian had hunted Tula, but she was swept into the protective embrace of the Sisterhood and Valya Harkonnen. Vorian himself had been murdered in the final confrontation in the ruins of Corrin. . . .

The blood feud was not over, and Willem didn't think it ever would be. But now that he saw Danvis Harkonnen dead, perhaps it was a good start.

One of the diplomats in the hall glared at him. "It's Willem Atreides! The Atreides killed him, just like he killed the other nobles!"

Willem's anger flashed. "I did nothing of the sort!"

Close beside him, Luc used his burly body to block any threat.

"Look at the rash on the body," the Suk doctor said, calmly yet accusingly. "Just like the previous three victims."

"I didn't kill them, either!"

A noblewoman in stiff skirts and ornamental shoulder pads huffed. "Yet, you are the one who stands to gain the most."

Willem heard vindictive muttering in the halls as sympathy turned toward the Harkonnens. Luc wrapped a beefy arm around him, herding him down the corridor. "Come, let's get away from here."

Willem called out, trying to make himself heard. "We will see Emperor Javicco about this! I swear on my Atreides honor that I'm not guilty!"

They rushed away, trying to get ahead of the rumors. Luc said in a low voice, "Your protestations might convince me and my family, but others do not hold Atreides honor in such high regard."

After they had retreated to Willem's private quarters in an adjacent wing, Luc summoned his companions to serve as an impromptu protective detail. The big man suggested that Willem lay low until the initial anger passed and medical studies could be performed on Danvis Harkonnen's body.

But Willem would have none of it. "No. Every second that passes, Emperor Javicco's opinion of me grows more and more poisoned. I must speak to him now, in the open throne room, and to anyone who wishes to listen!"

Luc popped a small fruit from a display bowl into his mouth. "If you ask me, you should just go with us to Kepler. You'll be welcome there for as long as you need to be."

"If I run, I will appear guilty."

"At least you'd be alive," said one of the women in the Atreides party, the field medic Eldira.

Willem scowled. "I will not tolerate living as a huddling exile. Come with me or stay here, as you wish." He pushed past the other Atreides, determined to face Javicco and explain himself.

With a melodramatic sigh, Luc gestured to his companions, and they all followed him down the tense palace corridors. The restless, angry murmur became a loud undertone as Willem pushed his way past the door guards and into the cacophony of the throne room.

Young Javicco sat like a pile of discarded gaudy clothes on the crystal throne. Choosing not to follow protocol, Willem marched forward without being announced. "Sire, I have been falsely accused." Luc Atreides and his ragtag entourage hurried behind him.

Startled and upset, Javicco leaned forward on his throne and glared at Willem. "Accused? That much is a fact, and I shall decide whether or not the charges are false."

Willem bowed deeply. "I serve you with my life, Sire. The rancor between Atreides and Harkonnen is well known after the generations of unspeakable crimes that House has inflicted upon mine."

"Crimes?" a shrill voice cried. "Crimes have been committed *against* Harkonnens."

A young man pushed forward, a whirlwind of fiery anger. Willem at first didn't recognize him, but he had a Harkonnen look about him, generous lips, a widow's peak—Gerhard Harkonnen, Danvis's cousin, a man who kept to the shadows and rarely entered the court spotlight.

Gerhard shouted to the crowd. "The Atreides disgraced my family name. The Atreides murdered Danvis's brother Griffin! And now you've killed him too, along with all your rivals." Imperial guards tried to intercept the young Harkonnen, but he flailed past them. "Atreides are the bloodthirsty ones here!"

Willem felt ice in the pit of his stomach, tried to remain calm. Ignoring Gerhard, he addressed the Emperor. "Again I insist, Sire—I had nothing to do with what befell Danvis Harkonnen or the other nobles."

"His cousins brought poison from Kepler!" someone else in the crowd shouted. Likely a Harkonnen plant.

Indignant, Luc scooped his young son into a protective grip, while the rest of his entourage stood ready to fight.

Javicco's expression was sour and disappointed. "Yet, thanks to these deaths, your competition for an influential court position is gone. Do you think now that you can advance into this role as my most trusted advisor? To be the mouthpiece of the Emperor himself, by simply killing off those who stand in your way?"

"I did not harm them, Sire," Willem shouted, then controlled himself. "I will fight with all my soul to protect the Imperium, but I will also fight to protect my honor."

"This man has no honor!" Gerhard pushed past the guards. More brightly garbed security men stood in his way, but their sympathies seemed against Willem as well.

Emperor Javicco reached a decision. "Due to the obvious evidence against you, Willem Atreides, I declare that your name shall be withdrawn from consideration as my new chamberlain. We will begin another round of interviews, and you will not be included." He rose from his throne, glowering down at Willem, who stood proud and unshakeable. "I shall set in motion an immediate inquiry and put you on trial. If you are truly innocent, you have nothing to fear."

Willem took a step backward, unwilling to surrender. "I have everything to fear, Sire, since my enemies have already planted evidence against me."

"Not good enough!" Gerhard shouted. "He killed my blood relative, and I will not let him manipulate Imperial courts, bribe witnesses, and corrupt the truth."

Furious, Willem turned to face him. "I have not—"

Then the young Harkonnen man astonished them all by whipping out a flechette pistol concealed in the folds of his purple garment. Swinging the needle weapon up, he howled, "Kanly! I declare kanly!"

Even before the first scream rang out in the crowd, Gerhard fired.

Luc Atreides was already reacting. He grabbed Willem's shoulder, spun him halfway around but could not protect him from the burst of deadly needles. The sharp projectiles ripped into his side. Willem coughed blood and fell into Luc's arms.

The big Atreides man wrapped his arms around him and began dragging him off. "All Atreides! To me now!"

Before Gerhard could fire the needle pistol again, an Imperial guard knocked the weapon out of his hand with a sharp blow.

"Make way, dammit!" Luc roared. "By the pit of hell, make way!"

The other Atreides bowled the terrified courtiers aside. Carried by his brethren, Willem Atreides slumped like a blood-soaked rag, the wound in the side of his chest was like a fleshy crater.

"Kanly," Luc growled. "We'll show them kanly."

IX

The darkness was filled with screams and laughter, which shifted to buzzing, and finally became a blur of light . . . and a voice.

"Ah, you are awake, Danvis. The antidote must have worked." A little snicker. "I am surprised, frankly."

Thoughts and memories circled just out of reach. Questions and confusion. The soft, gray light resolved itself into a face—a Harkonnen face. Gerhard.

Danvis blinked his eyes in an attempt to get more clarity, and the effort was extreme, like opening and closing a set of heavy doors. He tried to speak, but couldn't even remember how to breathe.

In and out, in and out. At last a hoarse noise came out of his throat.

"Now, now, you mustn't talk just yet, cousin."

Gerhard moved at the edge of his field of view, but Danvis couldn't move his eyes to look where the other man had gone, couldn't remember how.

"We're back in your private bedroom in the Harkonnen Consulate, resting in a comfortable chair," Gerhard explained, humming in an irritating way. "I know you preferred to spend time in your palace suite rather than here, but this is your real home. Harkonnen territory. A fitting place for your recovery."

He continued to pace, continued to explain. "One of the Suk doctors noticed that your life signs were faint and likely fading. As your grieving cousin, I wanted you to spend your final hours here." Gerhard stood in front of him, and clutched his hands over his heart in a mocking gesture of grief. "After your dire medical prognosis, I secretly administered a reviving stimulant, and soon you should be coming out of the catatonic state."

Danvis's thoughts cleared enough for him to remember the plan—the toxic inigo gnats, the harsh antidote . . . though he hadn't expected the effects to be so devastating.

Yes, he had done all this to destroy the reputation of Willem Atreides, and have him face Imperial execution.

He made a croaking sound again, and his cousin leaned closer in an attempt to hear. He clicked his tongue. "You are quite incomprehensible, Danvis. But I know which questions you're likely to ask." He brushed the front of his shirt. "Our plot is succeeding remarkably. When you fell victim to the heinous Atreides poisoning, the court went into a complete uproar—as expected. Willem was accused of the crime, and everyone of importance is convinced of his guilt."

Gerhard paced back and forth. "But I have added a little extra icing on the cake, a twist that even you didn't foresee."

Danvis still couldn't move, and none of it made sense to him. By now, he should be getting stronger, should be awakening. He tried to raise his hand, but barely felt a finger tremble. He blinked again, and his eyelids opened and closed with ponderous heaviness.

Gerhard's voice took on a mocking, superior tone. "You see, after your dying body was rushed away, my dear cousin, I was struck by such profound grief and anger. When Emperor Javicco himself accused the vile Atreides, I simply couldn't control myself. I howled and declared kanly." He laughed even louder. "Kanly! I pulled out a flechette pistol and shot Willem with a full blast of the needles."

As he struggled to speak again, Danvis was alarmed to feel wetness trickle down his cheek: drool coming out the side of his lips. The complex and articulate question in his mind emerged as nothing more than a gurgle.

"What's that? How did I bring the pistol into the Imperial court past the Emperor's security?" Gerhard mused. "Simple, since there was so much turmoil. The true suspicion was centered around Willem Atreides. I slipped in easily."

Danvis tried his other hand, and the little finger twitched. A pounding resonated inside his skull, and a red edge of pain lingered behind his vision. The unexpected wheaty smell of baking bread came to his nostrils, and soon wafted away. Was it just a sensory hallucination? Strange colors sparkled around his vision, which blurred and then sharpened again.

"Willem Atreides received a mortal wound, surely," Gerhard said. "Though I hope he doesn't die too quickly. I could have used poison on the needles to make certain he suffered a long and painful death—I'd have been justified in doing so."

He extended a cup of water toward Danvis, whose mouth hung open. "Here, have a sip." He gently dribbled the water into Danvis's mouth, then frowned in disgust. He bustled about the room until he came back with a cloth towel to wipe off his cousin's face. "You drool a bit too much for my taste. I hope you'll learn to control it . . . eventually."

Danvis struggled with the questions again. *Eventually?*

"After shooting the Atreides, I was apprehended, but my grief was palpable . . . and excusable. I know Imperial law, and I correctly declared kanly, even filed a proper brief before I entered the throne room, so I was completely within my rights after what Willem did to you. There will be an inquiry, of course, but I'll be cleared—especially since it will be proved that the craven Atreides poisoned you and all the others. He will die before he can raise any questions that I don't want raised."

Danvis made a louder groaning sound and saw lines furrowing his cousin's brow. "I'm afraid I can't understand you, Danvis, so I'll have to make my best guess. Someday if you recover enough motor control in your fingers, I could give you a stylus if you want to communicate. For now, you have nothing to worry about. Just take a rest."

Gerhard patted Danvis on the head as if he were some kind of pet, or child . . . or invalid. "Nothing to worry about. I will, of course, take your position at court. I promise to do my utmost to raise our family status and to whisper in the young Emperor's ear. After all the treachery in the Imperial court, he needs advice more than ever."

Danvis wanted to lunge out of the chair and throttle his cousin, but though he strained and twisted, his body only jerked. Soon, he began spasming uncontrollably. His arms flailed, his knees jittered in the chair, his head bobbed from side to side. Scarlet explosions appeared across his vision and inside his head. Pain wracked his entire body.

Gerhard looked inconvenienced rather than alarmed. "Oh dear, not another seizure." He grasped his cousin's shoulders and forcibly held him in place until the spasms subsided. Afterward, Danvis felt as if his muscles had been strained taut, and some had snapped like frayed cables.

Gerhard let out a concerned sigh. "I suppose I should call a Suk doctor to look at you, while I cry out with joy that you have escaped certain death! The medical experts will marvel at your miraculous recovery. No doubt they'll want to draw blood samples and run excruciating tests, but they'll find nothing. I, of course, will allow it because I would do anything to help you recover."

Danvis made a rattling sound in his throat.

"No, I didn't miscalculate the antidote." Gerhard sounded annoyed. "Even though detailed information about inigo toxin is limited, I knew what I was doing. Oh, perhaps I should have warned you of an unfortunate possible reaction. You see, poma juice can have an adverse effect on the antidote's efficacy. You probably shouldn't have consumed so much."

Danvis squirmed, listening in horror.

"You did survive the bites of the gnats, which was our intent." Gerhard rubbed his palms together gleefully. "Alas, you've had a stroke, perhaps several of them."

As he spoke, he walked around Danvis's chair. First, his cousin was in his field of view, then not visible, although his voice continued around behind the chair.

Then Gerhard reappeared in front of him. "Recovery is not likely, I'm afraid, but we will tend you with love and care, dear cousin, with all the resources of our noble family. I'm sure the Emperor himself will offer any necessary support."

Gerhard patted him on the shoulder. Danvis wanted to scream, but couldn't.

"From now on, I will take care of House Harkonnen."

X

Rushing out of the chaos of the throne room, Luc Atreides and his companions carried Willem's blood-soaked body toward the guest suites. Luc's niece Eldira had training in field medicine, and she pressed wadded rags against the gaping wound the flechette needles had torn into Willem's side, but it did little to stanch the blood flow.

As they paused at an intersection of corridors, Eldira looked up at Luc. "We have to get him someplace I can properly tend him."

Luc muttered, "Or at least where he can die in peace without gawkers."

Picking up the bleeding man, they rushed to the Atreides quarters, shouting ahead to clear the way. When they finally got Willem to his room, they stretched him out on the bed, where his blood oozed onto the sheets. He was pale and cold, still alive but just barely.

Eldira cut away Willem's tunic, exposing the wide wound. Blood kept pulsing up. "The needles tore through his flesh, and some of them penetrated deeper into the lungs. One may have nicked his heart."

Luc felt a wild rage inside him. Harkonnens! Harkonnens had done this. Someone must have planted evidence to frame Willem for poisoning the other nobles, and that cast aspersions on the entire Atreides line. Luc did not take such an insult lightly. He bent over Willem. "Hold on. You have to stay alive. You must watch what we'll do to the Harkonnens."

The other gathered Atreides muttered in agreement.

Luc looked at Eldira, seeking honesty, and she shook her head again. Willem's eyes were open, but they only stared into the distance. His face twisted in pain. He whispered, "Harkonnens . . . they can't—"

"Don't worry, we will have our revenge. We'll wipe out every last Harkonnen."

With great effort, Willem said, "No . . . this can't . . . go on . . . forever." He tried to sit up, which only caused more blood to pour out.

Luc physically held him down. "Rest now—don't exert yourself. You're not making sense."

But Willem seemed more clear-eyed than before. "Feud . . . has to stop!"

It took the last energy out of him, and he collapsed. In the deep open wound, the blood flow finally stopped. Luc squeezed his cousin's hand until he felt Willem's fingers tighten, then go limp. The eyes drifted shut, and the young nobleman rattled out his last breath.

Stunned at the loss, Luc remained motionless. Ranny stood close, leaning over the body, his eyes bright and full of anger. All of the Atreides gathered around.

Eldira looked helplessly at her bloody hands, devastated. "You heard what he said."

Luc drew a deep breath. "I heard nothing—nor did any of you."

"He said the feud must not go on forever!" she insisted.

"It will not go on forever, because we will eradicate the Harkonnens. We will find another way of ending it." The other family members looked on, staring at Willem's dead body, and then up at Luc.

"We are Atreides," he said.

Knowing the fallout that was sure to come—persecution from misinformed Imperials, accusations and detentions of anyone with the name of Atreides—Luc reached a decision. "We'd better depart for Kepler before anyone can stop us. We will take our cousin's remains with us." He felt sickened, enraged, and determined. "We don't belong here on Salusa Secundus."

XI

A cold fog blew in across the fjords of Lankiveil, and watery, pale sunlight struggled through the clouds overhead.

"Such a beautiful view, isn't it, Danvis?" Gerhard asked, expecting no answer.

Danvis had not been able to make an articulate response since the poisoning. He knew his cousin had botched the antidote on purpose. It was a power scheme worthy of . . . of a Harkonnen. He had to admit that, but the *way* he'd done it!

Suk doctors had poked and prodded him for interminable weeks to decipher the miracle of his recovery. Emperor Javicco had finally, sadly, declared there was nothing more they could do for poor Danvis, and he let Gerhard take him back home to the bleak world where Abulurd Harkonnen had been exiled nine decades earlier. *Home*.

The wind was cold out on the open patio, but Gerhard wrapped a fresh blanket around Danvis's lap and chest, covering his arms so no one could see him twisting and contorting his fingers, making feeble motions. Danvis was sure he could eventually communicate in this manner, perhaps making letters with finger movements, spelling out the guilt of Gerhard Harkonnen. But not if no one could see it.

He swore he would manage to get his revenge, somehow. But not soon. That would take a great deal of work.

Gerhard positioned the chair so that Danvis's slack-jawed face looked out at the fjords, the stark cliffs across the dull water. "I imagine you'd like to sit out here and ponder great ideas. What are you thinking inside that head of yours?" He rudely tapped Danvis on the forehead.

If Danvis had had a weapon of any kind—and if only his body could move—he would have slaughtered his cousin on the spot. . . .

The manor house was a modest structure compared to the Harkonnen Consulate on Salusa Secundus. But this was where Danvis had grown up with his sisters Valya and Tula, his brother Griffin, striving to drag their noble family out of the muck of disgrace.

Now, Gerhard commanded significant influence at the Imperial court, and he diverted substantial funds to Lankiveil. Objectively, Gerhard could accomplish much for their noble family, and undoubtedly he had been in touch—not admitting his own guilt of course—with Mother Superior Valya Harkonnen on Wallach IX.

Danvis thought that he hated his cousin more than he hated the Atreides. Could such a thing be possible? Yes, he thought so.

After the glib Gerhard finished positioning the chair, he called for the medical attendants who hardly ever left Danvis alone.

One of them checked Danvis's vitals, another adjusted the blanket, smiling close to his face. A third assistant arrived with a serving tray. "Some juice for you, sir." Lifting a squeeze bottle of cool poma juice, the matronly woman inserted the straw between her patient's lips and pushed, forcing the liquid into his mouth. He wanted to spit it back out, but the best he could do was to let it dribble from the side of his mouth. Now the tart taste of the drink repulsed him.

His little finger twitched.

The attendant clucked her tongue and fastidiously wiped the mess from his face.

"You have so few pleasures in life now, *cher* cousin," Gerhard said. "And I know how much you enjoy poma juice. I'll make certain they give it to you every day. The icing on the cake."

When the attendants left them again, Gerhard crossed his arms over his chest, radiant despite the fog and gloom of the fjords. "Every part of the plan worked perfectly, cousin. I'm sure you're proud of me, in your own way."

Danvis's finger moved, but not nearly enough to clench into a stranglehold. He seethed, but did not want to show it, although his eyes winced enough for Gerhard to recognize some of his displeasure.

"You must wish I had just killed you, yes? No? I guess I'll just have to interpret for myself. I studied our interesting family history, cousin—remember the words of our ancestor Xavier Harkonnen, the great hero of Serena Butler's jihad? He was talking about family love, and he stated unequivocally that a Harkonnen does not kill a Harkonnen."

Gerhard turned to look out at the gunmetal gray sea. "I followed his advice, but I used your tragic situation as leverage. Now House Harkonnen will grow even more powerful, thanks to you. History will call you a great martyr in our just cause."

He patted Danvis on the shoulder and forcibly gave him another sip of poma juice.

Danvis managed to twitch his finger again, a little more than before.

Acknowledgments

Special thanks to those who have helped us take a great journey through Frank Herbert's spectacular universe. Shawn Speakman, who encouraged us to write two of these four stories; our literary agents John Silbersack and Robert Gottlieb; Tom Doherty at Tor Books; and Kim Herbert and Byron Merritt at Herbert Properties LLC, who are dedicated to maintaining the Frank Herbert legacy.